# MEET YOUR MATCH, CUPID DELANEY

# MEET YOUR MATCH, CUPID DELANEY

## Ellen Leroe

LODESTAR BOOKS

Dutton     New York

Copyright © 1990 by Ellen Leroe

*Library of Congress Cataloging-in-Publication Data*

Leroe, Ellen, date
  Meet your match, Cupid Delaney / Ellen Leroe.—lst ed.
    p.   cm.
  Summary: A cupid-in-training who has been temporarily turned into a mortal girl faces her most difficult mission, to bring love and old-fashioned romance back to Woodside High in time for the junior-senior prom.
  ISBN 0-525-67309-1
  [1.  High schools—Fiction.  2.  Schools—Fiction.]  I.  Title.
PZ7.L5614Me  1990                     90-5896
[Fic]—dc20                                CIP
                                                AC

Published in the United States by Lodestar Books, an affiliate of Dutton Children's Books, a division of Penguin Books USA Inc.

Published simultaneously in Canada by Fitzhenry & Whiteside Limited, Toronto

Editor: Rosemary Brosnan

Printed in the U.S.A.

First Edition

10  9  8  7  6  5  4  3  2  1

*once more for Joy,*
*and for Merry Banks, prom queen forever and*
*Most Popular in everyone's yearbook*

# The Mission

Cupid Delaney was late.

The goddess and the bumblebee had been waiting for over an hour, and now Valentina Amour was ready to do something crazy. Hurl a lightning bolt into the center of the sleepy Woodside, New Jersey, community, freeze the carloads of shrieking, laughing teenagers who kept racing one another up and down the main street—in other words, behave in a most unseemly, ungoddesslike manner.

But that was Cupid Delaney for you. She somehow managed to get under your skin. She never did what was expected. She had a mind of her own. As sweet and innocent as she looked, she had spelled trouble as a cupid-in-training for the entire Northeast Love Bureau, but most of all for the Love Bureau's administrator, Valentina Amour herself. Today, however, the goddess would assign Cupid Delaney her last mission. She hoped Cupid Delaney would pass the test and finally fly up and earn her wings, getting the girl out of Valentina's domain and out of Valentina's hair.

From her perch behind some high, fluffy clouds, the Sweetheart Squad Leader peered down once again at the small shop-lined street. The fat black and yellow bumblebee that served as her companion—but was also a young male cupid—buzzed around her head.

"Are you sure she's coming?" he asked.

Valentina snorted. "I know that cupid inside and out, and she always walks home from school this way. She loves to window-shop. And she particularly loves Tatters, the women's dress boutique directly below us. There's no way we'll miss her."

The bee quivered in mid-flight. His black eyes fixed nervously on his superior's face. "I still feel funny about my part in the whole Cupid Delaney assignment. Are you sure she'll never find out who—or what—I really am?"

Valentina dismissed him with a wave of her hand. "Trust me. This is one Love Bureau trainee who won't have the time, or the energy, let alone the smarts, to figure out who's following her every move and why. Now relax, Andrew, and for Venus's sake, stop that incessant tuneless humming. It's beginning to annoy me—oh! Here she comes. Only an hour and ten minutes later than her normal time. Our little unsuspecting Cupid hopeful. And she's with her all-too-human and all-too-klutzy boyfriend, Alvin Danziger. What she ever sees in that carrot-top goofball is beyond me, but she failed her last mission primarily because of him."

Andrew stared curiously at the individual he had heard so much about through Love Bureau gossip. The girl had made history by bungling a mission and falling in love with her subject, sixteen-year-old Alvin Danziger. She had not been thrown out of the division, as everyone had expected. Instead, Valentina Amour had taken pity on the girl and granted her incredible wish of becoming a flesh-and-blood teenage mortal in the junior class for the re-mainder of the year at Woodside High. Now that time was almost up, and Cupid Delaney had no idea that a huge fist in the beauteous form of Valentina Amour was poised over her head, about to smash her perfect high school days into tiny bits. Cupid Delaney's romantic bubble was about to burst.

Valentina stood up abruptly, adjusting the folds of her diaphanous toga around her perfect figure. "Quickly, Andrew, into Tatters' front window where she'll see us."

A clap of her hands, a burst of shiny, confetti-colored smoke, and the two emissaries from the Love Bureau zapped into Tatters' display mannequins . . .

. . . just as Cupid Delaney and Alvin Danziger ambled into view. They were holding hands and smiling at each other.

Delaney walked slowly, yet with a bounce in her step, savoring the perfect mid-May weather. The sun poured down a butterscotch warmth, the birds chirped gaily, and some of the storefronts held wooden boxes crammed with a dazzling profusion of flowers. It was Friday afternoon, the prom was coming up, and all her thoughts were focused on the dance and how exciting it would be to attend her very first junior/senior prom.

Delaney sighed. Everything is perfect, she thought. If it gets any more perfect, I don't think I can stand it. I've got good grades this term, I'm friends with the three funniest and nicest girls at school and they let me join their private club, and now the prom is coming and I get to go with Alvin.

Alvin Danziger was string-bean lean, with tousled reddish-blond hair that drooped over horn-rimmed glasses. Boyish-featured, haphazardly dressed, a science and math whiz, he was not the epitome of high school cool. But there was a surprising warmth behind the vulnerable, awkward façade, a quirky sense of humor that set Alvin apart and made him special in Delaney's eyes.

In a burst of thankfulness, she squeezed Alvin's fingers and was rewarded by the lopsided grin that always melted her heart.

"What are you so twinkly about? Getting an A on that surprise quiz in English?"

"It's not the English test, and you know it. They announced that prom tickets are going on sale next week, and I can't wait to go."

Did the warmth in Alvin's affectionate smile cool a few degrees?

"Oh, no," he groaned. "Every time I turn around, hyperactive Woodside High is at it again, advertising yet another must-attend social event. Delaney, we've gone to every single mixer, rally, dance, and play since December, and I really don't think I have the energy to go to the most phony, the most pseudo-social happening of the combined junior/senior class. If you don't mind, I think I'll pass."

He'll *pass?* Was he serious? Miss the most romantic dance of the year? No, the puppy-dog eyes behind the dark horn-rimmed glasses were playful. He was teasing her again, and she had almost believed it.

"Had you going there, didn't I?"

She laughed in relief. "You sounded so gloomy! For a moment, well . . ."

Alvin impulsively picked her up and swung her around. "I hate to dance, I'm the world's worst, but I'd never pass up a chance to be with you."

"Oh, Alvin." Her heart melted. "That really means a lot."

And it did. Alvin had not been a big partygoer when she first met him last November, but he had really made an effort to please her by going to dances and on dress-up dates on weekends. Perhaps he had enjoyed expressing his carefully hidden romantic streak as much as an ex-cupid enjoyed expressing hers.

Watch it, Delaney, she warned herself. Don't even *think* the word *cupid*. If Alvin ever suspected the truth, her secret would be out. She'd probably find herself questioned by well-intentioned school counselors who wanted to "cure" her delusion! But Alvin's memory of that fateful week in November had been distorted by the intervention of the Love Bureau. He now thought he had met Delaney at the Homecoming Grid as a new (and very normal) teenage girl in the school. Yet she wasn't a normal teenage girl, not even now. The memories, powers, and associations connected to the Love Bureau were too strong. Delaney had always been a valentines-and-lace, red-rose romantic in matters of the heart. Alvin's idea of a good time on a date had formerly been chess games, evenings at the library, or explaining the mechanics of a motor in all its grease-drenched glory. Opposites must attract, because Alvin and Delaney got along beautifully. And now, thought Delaney, the prom would bring them even closer together as a couple.

But before she could get out another word, a slight breeze ruffled her curly blonde hair, and she heard a whisper in the air that made her freeze.

"Cupid. Cupid Delaney."

*Cupid Delaney.* No one had addressed her in that manner in nearly six months. Delaney, who had been standing almost hypnotized, took a step back and then looked into Alvin's face.

He stood there perfectly still, regarding her blankly, not even blinking. Just like a statue. She waved a hand in front of those unseeing eyes. Yes. He *was* a statue. And that meant—

"Cupid Delaney," the voice whispered again, this time a trifle impatiently. "Over here."

It was coming from the front window of Tatters dress shop. But it couldn't be. There was no one inside the big display case except a male and female mannequin, dressed in the latest fashionable evening attire. Yet the dress the female mannequin had on was a silvery, almost irridescent toga that seemed to ripple in lifelike folds around the mannequin's body. It resembled something a goddess would wear . . .

A goddess.

Even as Delaney put two and two together, an eyelid of the exquisite, dark-haired mannequin drooped at her once, in a playful wink.

"Valentina Amour!" Delaney cried.

The goddess came to life and put a restraining finger to her lips.

"Not so loud, by Zeus! You want to wake up the entire town? Step closer to the window."

"But won't everyone notice you?"

"You've been away from the Love Bureau too long; that's for sure. No one will see me as anything other than a store dummy. But the first matter of business we must attend to is that carrot-top friend of yours."

"Alvin?"

"The very same. Send him home or to the library. Or back to whatever studious cave he inhabits. We can't have him standing in the middle of the sidewalk with that frozen fish stick expression on his face."

"Yes, but—"

Before Delaney could utter another word, Valentina snapped her fingers. The spell was lifted. The red-haired boy blinked, and looked around in a daze.

"Delaney? What happened?"

She took his arm. "Nothing. Look, Alvin, I want to go inside Tatters and try some dresses on, so why don't you go on home? I'll probably be hours and hours."

He winked at her. "Trying to get rid of me?"

"Yes, I mean no! Of course not! It's just that I'm looking for a dress for the prom and I don't want you to see what I pick out. I want it to be a surprise."

He was disappointed but accepted her story. Before he turned to go, however, he made a face and hit his forehead.

"Wait a minute. Wait just one minute. If you're looking for fancy dresses at Tatters, does this mean I'll have to rent a tux and wind up resembling a petrified penguin?"

Delaney gave him a grin and a little push. "Good-bye, Alvin."

"Hey, I was just kidding, or was I really? I mean, I'd look pretty silly in a tux, and I never was the suave, ultra-cool type, and—"

"Good-bye, Alvin."

He gave her a half-teasing, half-pleading grin before kissing her and loping down the street. Halfway down the block he looked back to see if she was still watching him. When he saw she was, he flapped his arms like a penguin and began to waddle.

Despite herself, Delaney had to laugh. Alvin Danziger was a character, all right. There was no one else in the entire junior class like him, quirks and all.

"And thank Jupiter for that," Valentina said wryly. She had obviously read Delaney's mind, and Delaney blushed. "What you see in that socially primitive nerd is beyond even my infinite capacities in matchmaking, but that's a subject we need not discuss at this time. Suffice it to say that there is a lesson to be learned from your, ah, relationship with Danziger, but a lesson you need to learn

7

on your own. Right now there's a more important topic to be discussed. Discussed and decided. Your future."

All the laughter died inside Delaney. She felt her stomach contract, her heart begin to pound. Realizing that her junior year at Woodside was nearly over, she had been waiting for the blow to fall—the summons from the Love Bureau. But what she would hear, what had been decided about her fate, was a question she almost didn't want answered. Cupid Delaney was confused, half a red-blooded, completely functional sixteen-year-old teenage girl, who thrived on books and study dates and soap operas and caring about friends and the environment, but half a cupid in mindset and personality and magic powers. A year ago, if Valentina had approached her to discuss her future, she wouldn't have had a single doubt about what she wanted that future to hold: a career as a Wing Level 3, Certified Love Bureau Cupid.

But that was a year ago. Before high school days and shopping malls and root beer floats and afternoons with her girl friends.

Before meeting and dating Alvin.

Delaney swallowed and tried to smile into the beautiful but piercing green eyes of the goddess who would determine her fate. She hoped that Valentina had not been tuning in to her private thoughts just now.

"What have you decided, Sweetheart Squad Leader?"

Valentina hestitated, glancing almost furtively across at the handsome but wooden-featured male mannequin. Then she tossed back her thick dark hair.

"Cupid Delaney, despite the fact that you have failed two out of three training assignments and broken the Cupid Code by falling in love with one of your subjects on the third assignment, the Love Bureau has decided to give you one more chance. I will assign you one final test, and if you manage to complete the test successfully, you will automatically fly up and receive your graduate Cupid wings."

"A final test? You mean right now?"

"What were you expecting, next Halloween? Next Groundhog Day? Of course right now," Valentina snapped. "Perhaps you've forgotten, but I granted you a school term at Woodside High, and come May twenty-sixth, that term will be up."

Delaney's eyes widened in dismay. "But May twenty-sixth? That's the date of the prom!"

"Exactly. And that's the assignment you'll be working on, Woodside High's junior/senior prom."

Delaney opened her mouth, but nothing came out. Her thoughts (and now her all-too-human teenage emotions) were in a whirl. What was wrong with her? She was being given a reprieve. A chance to earn her wings. Cupidhood was a viable opportunity.

So why did she feel so upset?

Because in order to gain that one prize, she'd have to let go of the other—her wonderful, carefree life as a Woodside High student. She wanted both. However, that was impossible. She had to choose.

She straightened up and tried to inject enthusiasm into her voice, but some confusion came through. "What will my mission be? It can't be too difficult because the prom's all set and the tickets go on sale next week."

"Not too difficult? NOT TOO DIFFICULT?" The goddess gave each word a distinct, sarcastic emphasis. Her eyes flashed. "You, of all people, should know me better than that. This mission is extremely important—and *very* difficult, I might add—not only to me, but to a certain other celestial being we will not mention by name, but whose powers far surpass mine and the other Love Bureau administrators and personnel."

Delaney's mouth dropped open. When she spoke, her voice came out a whisper. "You mean the Great Love Goddess herself . . . has an interest in Woodside High?"

"You may not realize it, but this prom at Woodside symbolizes the attitude of teenagers everywhere toward romance, candlelight, and all things relating to Valentine's Day. And the powers that be are strongly concerned that the current trends at your school indicate a lessening of interest in the old-fashioned values of love and romance."

"But that's crazy! That's not true. I'm sure lots of kids are planning to go!"

Valentina sighed. "I've looked into my heart-shaped crystal, Cupid Delaney, and let me tell you, everything's not as rosy as you so naively think. There is trouble brewing with the upcoming Woodside prom, a wrong slant being assigned to the theme and purpose behind it. Unless you get to work on correcting these two things and getting the junior and senior classes actively involved, it may turn out to be a disaster. And need I remind you, if the prom turns out to be a disaster, your dream of flying up and becoming a cupid turns out to be a disaster, too. And then, I'm afraid, there is nothing more I can do except boot you unceremoniously out of the Love Bureau, once and for all. That's crudely but honestly put. You'll be on your own."

Cold words. Frightening words. Delaney shivered despite the mild spring temperature. She had never been out on her own before, had only known the comforting, rosy-hued world of the Love Bureau, with its "Love Is All You Need" needlepoint wall hangings and cherubic friends and romantic Muzak selections piped nonstop throughout the complex. Delaney loved being a teenage girl, but she couldn't survive in her new world without Valentina Amour's help. What would she do for money? Where would she live? What would her future be?

During her school term, the Love Bureau had provided Delaney with a completely new identity, impeccable transcripts from out-of-state schools, and a picture-perfect rented home in Woodside and picture-perfect parents (who just happened to be an attractive forty-year-old cupid couple on temporary assignment). Every night Delaney and her playacting mother and father would settle in front of the VCR to review tapes of "normal" families, and as a result, Delaney's home life was a little too warm and welcoming, a little too much like scenes from a Disney movie. But kids never noticed anything amiss at her house.

"I wish my parentiles were as nice and as easygoing as yours," they'd exclaim enviously after being plied with heart-shaped, homemade chocolate chip cookies by Delaney's "mom."

Delaney outwardly had the perfect parents, the perfect home, even the perfect wardrobe, graciously supplied by Valentina Amour, but take away that magical backing of the Love Bureau, and where would she be?

Really and truly all on her own. It was too frightening to contemplate.

At that moment Delaney made up her mind. She'd throw her considerable energy and enthusiasm and magical powers into accomplishing her final mission. And when she finally reached full cupid status (well, there was no question about it. She had to pass this last assignment; she just *had* to!), she would look back at her glorious days at Woodside High with a private smile and a few nostalgic tears. But those days would be memories.

"Anything else you need to tell me about my assignment, Squad Leader Amour?" Delaney's face had cleared and brightened. There was an almost jaunty line to her posture.

Valentina laughed. "I see the Cupid Delaney I know so well is back, ready to tackle any obstacles, determined to win. But a word of warning, if I may. This mission is a tricky one. You won't be doing anything as easy as matching couples together or giving one shy person the courage to ask someone out on a date. We're not talking about one or two people, but an entire segment of Woodside High. You'll be working on the combined junior and senior classes, and that's well over eight hundred kids. And you won't be focusing on matchmaking, but on changing their attitudes. It's not as simple as you seem to think, judging by the look on your face."

"Not simple, no, but surely with the use of my magic powers, I—"

The goddess raised a hand, abruptly cutting Delaney off. "I meant to make this a difficult mission, and so I have. Cupid Delaney, you must go about your task without using any of your powers or special abilities—ever. If we catch you slipping or cheating and using any one of the numerous spells or enchantments, you will automatically fail the test and will be ordered to leave the Love Bureau at the conclusion of your mission."

"Not use my power? My magic?" Delaney demanded in a horrified voice. "But then how can I—? Whatever can I—?"

"It's amazing what a cupid trainee can come up with once she puts her mind to work and uses all the training she has received from her teachers at the Love Bureau."

"But—"

"Not to mention the experience—and dare I say the *wisdom*—she has gathered as a mortal teenage girl. Mix all these ingredients together and make them work for you. Bring love and old-fashioned romance back to Woodside High in time for the prom. Get the students behind you. Make our Great Goddess proud! I know you can do it, Cupid Delaney."

"But today's the eleventh. The prom's on the twenty-sixth. That only gives me two weeks!"

"All the better; you can get to work immediately. Now I really must be going. I'm helping an advertising agency with its Zeus Juice campaign, a marvelous ambrosial new drink, nonalcoholic yet with the kick of champagne . . ."

"Wait, Valentina! Please don't go. I've got so many questions . . ."

"Trust in yourself, Cupid Delaney. You have all the answers."

The goddess's chiseled features seemed to soften as she regarded her most troublesome cupid trainee, but before she vanished, a saleslady led a plump and perspiring customer up to the mannequin.

"Now here's the latest look this year, the Grecian toga. The height of fashion and very dramatic, don't you agree?"

The customer, sniffing in disapproval, reached out to stroke the folds of sheer fabric. "More like tasteless, if you want my opinion. Any woman who dares to wear this flimsy number in public is no lady—ouch!" She yanked back her hand in shock and pain. "Something pinched me! I tell you, something or some*one* pinched me!"

"Let me assure you, madam"—the saleslady drew herself up haughtily—"*I* did not pinch you. And if I did not pinch you, no one did."

Squabbling now, the two women went in search of the store manager while Valentina burst into mischievous laughter. "Insufferable female mortal. Serves her right,

*13*

telling a goddess she's not a lady. And now, Cupid Delaney, I really must fly."

With a slight flash of smoke and a pop, Valentina departed, leaving the blank-featured shell of the mannequin behind.

Delaney stared forlornly into the shop window. Two weeks to work a miracle at Woodside High. And she didn't have a clue as to what that miracle would turn out to be. She didn't have a clue about anything. With a sigh, Delaney turned and walked slowly down the street, failing to notice the bright black and yellow bumblebee that followed her like a shadow.

# Saturday Night Dreamers

"Will the Saturday Night Dream Club now come to order. When I call your name, please respond. And no funny comments. Courtenay Wilcox?"

"Here. But do we really need to call the roll with only four members in the club? It always seems so silly when you do it!"

"This is parliamentary procedure, as silly as it seems to you. To continue the roll. Pammi Gittner? Let the record show Pammi Gittner is responding to her own roll call and ignoring the outburst from Courtenay Wilcox, who should know better by now than to constantly interrupt the president when she's beginning a meeting. Now then, Helen Mapes? Let the record show that Helen called earlier and said she'd be a little late. Delaney Smith?"

Lengthy pause. Some throat clearing.

"Delaney Smith? Is Delaney here in physical form only or having an out-of-body experience?"

Sitting cross-legged on the living room rug, Delaney belatedly looked up and caught Pammi's eye. "What? Oh, sorry. Here."

"But is she really here," Pammi mused, "or in some other planetary dimension?"

"Oh, for pity's sake, I'm here, I'm here, I'm really here!" Delaney grabbed one of the heart-shaped pillows scattered around her and hurled it at her friend.

But she wasn't. Not really here properly. Not in her perfect Woodside home. Pammi was right. Ever since the visit from Valentina yesterday afternoon, all Delaney could think about was her assignment of the junior/senior prom. And what made it all the more confusing was that she hadn't the first idea where to start or what to do.

I'll come up with something, Delaney vowed. I really will. But in the interim I'm not giving up my Saturday night club. Saturday night meant only one thing to Delaney and her three best friends: the Saturday Night Dream Club. Every weekend without fail, the four girls met at five P.M. at one another's houses to watch the tape of their favorite soap opera, "The Young Dreamers." Tonight was Delaney's turn to play hostess.

"The Young Dreamers" was the most popular daytime entertainment on TV, thanks in part to exciting, cliffhanging story lines and to the looks and acting ability of the incredibly charismatic and sexy lead star, Storm Devrie. "Young Dreamers" aired at two o'clock, when the girls were still in school, but videotaping every show enabled them to get together on Saturday night to enjoy the full five hours of the melodramatic saga—and to ooh and aah over their favorite teen actor and dream man, Storm. Delaney had been a virtual stranger to soap operas when she entered Woodside High, but the ever-bubbling cauldron of love, hate, and other primitive emotions on "Young Dreamers" had quickly appealed to her cupid personality. She had eagerly agreed to join the Saturday Night Dream Club and found herself with mini-crushes, not only on Storm Devrie, but also on the two other teen

*16*

actors playing his best friend and brother on the show, Chad Collier and Mark Hall.

But Storm Devrie was the prime attraction. The girls collected articles about him, wrote to the show requesting autographed photos, and were the first in line at the record store when his enormously popular album came out a month ago. The hit single, "Dream Only of Me," a romantic ballad, had soared to the top of the music charts and was number one for the second straight week. If the kids at school didn't recognize Storm from his TV soap, they inevitably recognized him from his music and MTV video. His picture was pinned up in many lockers, but as far as Delaney knew, the Saturday Night Dream Club was the only local fan club devoted exclusively to him.

Normally, on Saturday nights all talk would focus around heartthrob Storm Devrie and the show's story line, but tonight Delaney couldn't concentrate.

"Listen, have either of you heard anything about the prom?"

Petite, softly rounded, always-wisecracking Pammi scrunched up her expressive features. "Prom? Did you say the word *prom?* Sorry. It doesn't compute. Could you spell that for me? It's been so long since I've attended a social function at school that I've forgotten what it means."

Courtenay, who was delicate-boned, with chin-length honey-gold hair, and was an eternal pessimist, shrugged. "Why should I even bother to find out anything about it? I know I won't be invited."

Pammi rounded on her with an incredulous laugh. "You amaze me, Wilcox, you really do. I know so many guys who would love to take you to the prom, but you wouldn't give them the time of day."

"They're not my type."

"And you're telling me Mitch Rhyner is not your type? Girl, he is *everyone's* type!"

"That's the problem, nuthead. He's everyone's type, and females of all shapes, sizes, and ages swarm around him like little kids around peanut butter. I could never get involved with someone like him. Besides, he never asked me out."

"He did, too! You don't call being invited to Streamers, Woodside's hottest night spot, a date?"

Courtenay's eyes flashed. "The only reason he asked me to go was because his band's keyboard player got sick and he knows I play keyboard and he just wanted me at Streamers in case the owner let his band audition."

"And you didn't go."

"I didn't go," Courtenay said with a defiant set to her jaw. "I refuse to fall all over Mitch Rhyner just like everyone else at Woodside High."

Delaney couldn't resist a desire to matchmake. "He likes you, Court," she said softly. "He really does. Why not give him a chance and treat him like a person instead of some phony, heartbreaking playboy?"

Pammi jumped up and clapped her hands. "Hear, hear! The voice of romance has spoken. And I agree with her. One hundred percent. Give the guy a chance."

"The way you give Tim a chance?"

"The Bratt! Surely you jest."

"I jest not. All you ever talk about is Timothy Bratt."

"Because I work for Mr. Gucci, the Preppie King. I slave for him. He's on my back all the time for copy for the school *Bulletin*. Can I help it if he drives me crazy and I mention his name to let off steam?"

"He drives you crazy because you like him," Delaney grinned.

Pammi crossed her eyes at Delaney. "Oh, you. Princess

*18*

of Romantic Notions. To you everyone secretly likes some-one. You're always aiming to fix us up. You think Mr. Rights are a dime a dozen."

"No, they're not, but I do believe they exist. And I think both of you have already located yours, only you're too afraid to do anything about it."

"Timothy Bratt the Third is so far from being anyone's conception of Mr. Right, it isn't funny. He's an obnox-ious, supercilious guy who never sweats, loves to give orders, and looks like someone stuck a coat hanger up his back. And you know what's worse? He never laughs. The big blue-eyed trout has absolutely no sense of humor whatsoever."

"Maybe if you stopped making fun of him and tried to talk to him normally, without all the jokes, you'd discover a vulnerable, sweet guy inside (or outside) the coat hanger," Delaney suggested. "Anyway, we weren't dis-cussing school politics, fashions, or the freezer section of your love life. We were talking about the prom."

"Well, exc-u-use me." Pammi threw herself onto the soft leather sofa and hugged one of the leather cushions. "I thought it was all painfully obvious to you, Princess of Romantic Notions. Your good buddies here don't know *nada* about the prom. Zero. Zip. Zilch. And anyway, what's the sudden interest? Isn't it a given that you and Alvin are going?"

"Well, yes, but . . ."

"But what?" Pammi demanded. "Why the hesitation? And why the weird faraway attitude tonight?"

"Hey, Delaney, what is it?" Courtenay's normally wor-ried expression turned even gloomier. "You didn't have a fight with Alvin, did you?"

Pammi jerked a finger at Delaney and giggled. "Her? Miss Sunshine and Perpetual Bubbling Spirits? No way.

*19*

Now can we *please* get down to the most important business of the day and decide what we're eating tonight? I'm
starving, and it always takes a half hour for anyone to
deliver if we're going to order Chinese or pizza."

Mrs. Smith, Delaney's cupid mother, wafted in from
the kitchen as if on cue. A scent of some heavenly fra-
grance wafted in with her. The attractive blonde woman
beamed down at the three girls with an angelic smile on
her face.

"Did I hear dinner being mentioned? Why, I could
whip something up for you in a moment. As soon as I
finish practicing the harp."

Harp lesson? This sounded (and *smelled*) entirely too
much like the Love Bureau. Delaney grimaced and caught
her "mother's" eye.

"Uh, thanks, but no thanks, Mom. We decided we want
pizza, I think."

Mrs. Smith let out a peal of laughter that sounded like
silver bells. In her cherry-red apron and white lacy dress,
she resembled an illustration from a Valentine's Day card.

"Pizza? Is that what teenage girls always eat for dinner?
Why, I never realized . . ."

Delaney hurriedly stood up. "How about making us
dessert, Mom? That angel food cake?"

"Hey, yes! Your cake is the greatest, Mrs. Smith!"
Pammi chimed in. "It's out of this world!"

You don't know how far out it really is, Delaney
thought. Mrs. Smith turned and wafted back into the
kitchen.

The girls called out for pizza and set up snack trays in
front of the VCR. Mrs. Smith bustled in once or twice,
making sure her "daughter's" guests were taken care of
and offering fruit juice, coffee, or milk to go with the

pizza. She brought in the drinks and then left, promising to return with the cake as soon as it was done.

Pammi looked at her watch and made a face. "I hope Helen gets here before the pizza arrives. She'll kill us if we start without her. Or if she misses a minute of 'Young Dreamers.' "

A few moments later they heard a strange blatting sound.

Delaney jumped up. "That's Alvin's horn!"

"The guy can't keep away from you," Pammi marveled.

The girls went to the large open window. Sure enough, Alvin had pulled up to the curb in his antiquated yellow VW, but it was a short, stocky, athletic-looking girl who stepped out of the passenger side. Dark tangles of hair fell untidily around her snub-nosed face.

"Helen," Pammi observed in a surprised tone of voice. She looked at Delaney. "He brought Helen here."

"Well, Helen and Alvin know each other. They're not strangers, for heaven's sake. There's nothing wrong with friends giving each other rides."

"Oh, yeah, sure," Pammi quickly said.

"Of course," Courtenay agreed. "Nothing wrong. Except . . ."

"Except what?" Delaney asked. "That you didn't think they were friends?"

Courtenay and Pammi exchanged guilty glances and nodded. To tell the truth, Delaney thought with a slight inward start, I didn't think the two were such bosom buddies myself.

Not after that fateful week in November.

Alvin and Helen had been a hot item at school first term. They had been seen doing everything together. Alvin had been crazy about Helen—until Cupid Delaney's third and disastrous mission at Woodside High.

21

Delaney had been ordered to match two unlikely couples in time for the November homecoming dance: shy and scholarly junior Helen Mapes with senior football star Craig Lacrosse, and eccentric nerd Alvin Danziger, Helen's devoted boyfriend, with the glamorous and oh-so-popular senior cheerleader, Dawn Cummings. You would think that the low-profile junior couple would give anything to date the two most exciting seniors at school, but Alvin gave Cupid Delaney the most trouble. He simply would not succumb to any of her spells to make him fall for Dawn Cummings. He remained faithful to his chess club partner and library date, Helen. Helen, however, was a different story. Cupid Delaney realized that although the seemingly colorless junior liked Alvin, she secretly yearned to walk into the homecoming dance on the arm of Craig Lacrosse. In a series of mishaps and some triumphs, too, Cupid Delaney granted Helen's wish and ordered Craig Lacrosse to fall under Helen's spell. The star quarterback was so smitten by Helen that he forced Dawn Cummings to elect her to the supremely elite Spirit Club, composed of senior movers and shakers in the school.

The ending to the Alvin Danziger story contained a twist. Cupid Delaney had broken all the rules and fallen in love with him herself. And once he saw that Helen wanted to date Craig, he turned to Cupid Delaney. But not all the endings were happily ever after. Because Love Bureau spells only last thirty days, Craig became disenchanted with Helen just before Christmas and resumed dating his beautiful but empty-headed admiring females. Helen had been crushed but had retained her position in the Spirit Club. Once elected, you could not be thrown out of the sacred inner circle of seniors. But the nine other members barely tolerated her, and Helen carried a major torch for Craig.

It had not ended happily for Helen. But it had ended happily for Alvin. And for Cupid Delaney, too, of course. Although, staring at Alvin, who had just jumped out of the car to talk to Helen, Delaney wondered. Alvin and Helen looked so *right* together. Delaney had forgotten how the two seemed to complement each other perfectly.

Pammi rapped sharply on the glass. Almost guiltily, Alvin looked up. Catching sight of the three girls, his face cleared. Both he and Helen grinned and waved. Alvin's smile was aimed directly and solely at Delaney. Delaney's spirits lifted. Just be happy Alvin and Helen are renewing their friendship, she thought.

"Did you start yet?" Helen yelled.

"We're waiting for you," Courtenay yelled back. "And the pizza's just arrived, right behind you. That's what I call great timing!"

"I'll be right there." Helen murmured something to Alvin and hurried up the front steps, while inside the living room . . .

. . . *the bumblebee crawling along the bottom of the flower vase froze in sudden agitation. A mass of yellow, black-eyed daisies made for perfect camouflage, so he had not worried about being seen by the three girls, but now he realized he had to make a move. His extra-perceptive sensitivity to all things concerning Cupid Delaney's mission told him that a key person with some answers to her problem was walking through the front door and into the living room. But how to steer Cupid Delaney in the right direction?*

*Even as he inched slowly from behind the protection of the vase, someone slammed a glass of juice down on the table, almost squashing him flat. The impact made him jump into the air and land on his back. Angrily he twitched his wings and righted himself.*

*This was a rotten thing he was doing, Andrew thought. This was a rotten job. Being ordered to spy on Cupid Delaney to see that she did not use her powers. He understood the reason behind the onerous task, but he didn't have to like it. And he liked it even less after viewing Cupid Delaney for the first time Friday. Valentina Amour had described the cupid trainee as some charming monster, a troublemaker and rebel par excellence. But Cupid Delaney resembled a monster about as much as a newborn kitten. In fact, peering at her now, Andrew realized she had a kittenish look about her, with softly slanted blue-gray-green eyes, uptilted button nose, golden hair, and a smile that called to mind a little angel in a second-grade production of the Nativity. She smiled often and warmly, and how Valentina could call this attractive teenage girl a troublemaker was beyond him, but orders were orders. Andrew had to keep an eye on Cupid Delaney for the next two weeks and that was that.*

*But he could help her, too, couldn't he? Nothing so major it could be misconstrued as disobedience by Squad Leader Amour. Nothing to get Cupid Delaney in trouble. Just a friendly little push, to get her looking in the right places. Praying eagle-eyed Valentina wasn't monitoring his action right now from the Love Bureau viewing room, Andrew took a deep breath, heard his plump body automatically begin the humming preparatory to flying, and, shall we say, made a beeline straight toward the girl who had the answers—*

Delaney saw the fattest bumblebee in the world dive-bomb Helen Mapes and, all at once, Pammi and Courtenay screamed, the pizza delivery man froze while counting his change, while the helpless victim ducked and dropped her purple canvas book bag. Books, papers, and pens spilled across the floor. Luckily, the bee only brushed Helen's hair and flew straight out the open window.

"Did you see that? Did you see that—that gigantic thing!" Courtenay demanded. "Helen, it didn't sting you, did it?"

Helen managed to shake her head and smile. Delaney knelt and helped Helen pick up the scattered contents of the book bag: schedules of the chess club get-together with West Orange High, a school newspaper, homework assignments from advanced algebra and chemistry, pale pink note cards scribbled in purple ink, detailing arrangements about the junior/senior prom—

The *prom*. Here were a dozen or more cards giving every detail imaginable about theme, funding, entertainment, tickets, and hotels for the May 26 function. Delaney cradled the pink and purple-lined paper with the same excited reverence as Moses handling the stone tablets up on the mountain. Here was the answer, placed almost miraculously into her lap. She was so excited that she failed to hear a slight self-congratulatory humming sound coming from the windowsill. If she'd looked up, she would have found friendly black bumblebee eyes gazing directly at her.

She helped Helen stuff all the other papers and books back into the bag while Courtenay and Pammi sliced the steaming pizza. Before they sat down, though, she held up the incredible evidence before Helen's eyes.

"Helen, these note cards. How come you have information about the prom in your bag?"

"Note cards? What are you talking about?" She turned a startled face toward Delaney. Then she examined one of the pink note cards more closely and gave a cry.

"What are Claire's cards doing in my bag? Look, see the faint monogram on top? These are Claire Reggio's, but how did they ever get mixed up in my stuff . . ." Helen thought a moment, then snapped her fingers. "Un-

*25*

less Claire somehow mistakenly inserted them into the Spirit Club minutes. She's president this term and I'm secretary, so I record all the Spirit Club business."

Secretary. Minutes. Spirit Club business. That was a good one. No one laughed or made fun of Helen's little deception, however, because no one wanted to hurt her feelings. Everyone in the Saturday Night Dream Club knew all too well that the snobby members of the Spirit Club called Helen secretary in only the vaguest sense of the word. If she sat in on any meetings at all, it was rare and only out of the necessity to take down official school business. Primarily the studious girl "helped" them with difficult class assignments or research for English or history papers they were too lazy or unintelligent to do themselves. And Helen put up with it all—the drudgery, the grunt work—because it kept her linked to the golden circle of Woodside High, the top rungs of the social hierarchy. Not to mention the fact that Craig was a member of the club, and she could sit across the table from him and feast those wistful eyes of hers on his larger-than-life movie-star looks. It was sad and disturbing to her friends that Helen had not waked up to the insincerity and mindlessness of these senior Titans, but it was Helen's life and Helen's choice to make a fool of herself if she wanted to. They only wished she'd come to her senses one of these days and resign from the Spirit Club.

"You mean you didn't know that the Spirit Club was running the prom this year?"

Delaney regretted the words once they were spoken, but she was far too shocked—and more than a little suspicious—to spare her friend's feelings. Why would the Spirit Club keep something as ordinary as organizing the prom a secret? What devious plot could they be hatching?

"Back to the prom again," Pammi said, casting a puzzled glance at Delaney. "What's with this obsession with the prom? Will someone please tell me? Anyway, I'm starved. I'm going to start eating. Anyone else care to join me?" She sank into her seat and bit into a slice of pizza.

Courtenay sat down, too, but ignored the food. "What *is* going on, Delaney? Why all the questions about the prom?"

"Yeah," Helen chimed in, trying to regain some semblance of dignity after Delaney's tactless remark. "What's the big deal?"

Delaney stared at the cards and then around the circle of interested faces. Be careful, an inner voice whispered. Don't let anything slip as to your real identity—or these girls will be dialing the mental health hotline pronto. "Yes, we have a strange case to report. Our teenage friend claims she's a real-life cupid, yes, the kind with bows and arrows and little white wings. You will? You'll see her right after you see the man who swears he's Captain Hook? Oh, thank you! We'll bring her in."

She had to watch her step. But at the same time, she had been given a mission to fulfill. Perhaps a Mission Impossible. In order to pass it, she might need the help of her three best friends. Lord knew, she couldn't use magical resources to carry it off. She had to use human ones and hope for the best. She skimmed over Claire's note cards and gasped. No wonder Valentina had warned her about the upcoming prom. If ever there had been a less romantic theme for a dance, she didn't know what it could be. Romance? The Spirit Club was showing how they felt about romance. It was a slap in the face to the Love Bureau, and to the Great Love Goddess herself.

"For heaven's sake, what is it?" demanded Pammi. "You're reading those stupid cards like the answers to our exams were written on them."

"I wish," Courtenay sighed.

"No, not exam answers," Delaney said softly. "Something more revealing. Claire's listed the prom's theme, color, song, flower, motto—all decided for us, mind you. We don't even get a chance to vote."

"Most of the kids don't really care," Courtenay said with a shrug. "Sorry, but that's the way our school feels about the prom. Last year it was so bad that it lost money. Hardly anyone came to it."

"Yeah, I heard that it might be canceled this year," Pammi said. "It surprised me that we're even having one."

Delaney rustled the note cards angrily. "Well, I think you'll be even more surprised once you hear what the Spirit Club has planned for the dance. Just listen to the theme: Mogul Madness, or Puttin' on the Glitz. Official prom song, or wait, we have two warm and sentimental songs to choose from: Madonna's 'Material Girl' and Randy Newman's 'It's Money That Matters.' "

Pammi burst into laughter. "It's a joke, right? Your odd sense of humor?"

Delaney's lips tightened. "No joke. The choice of prom colors will tell you that: green and silver. Appropriate, isn't it? Green for dollar bills and silver for coins. Oh, and in case we don't get it, the motto is 'Reach for the stars . . . and carry a platinum American Express card.' Touching, isn't it?"

"Touching? It's revolting!" yelled Pammi. She bit into the pizza with loud, angry crunches.

"And the second romantic motto: 'High on life . . . bullish on the stock market.' "

Pammi choked while Courtenay jumped up to pat her on the back.

"Are you all right?" Helen asked.

"All right! How can I be all right after hearing all that

28

garbage?" Pammi growled. "I can't believe it! Delaney, you're making it up!"

Delaney flipped the card onto Pammi's tray. "Read it yourself. I don't have the imagination to create this stuff. But what's even worse is the proposed budget for entertainment and hotel. She wants to rent the most exclusive, most expensive place in northern New Jersey—the Crystal Springs Country Club, ten thousand dollars for the banquet room and three hundred dollars per couple for dinner. And entertainment? Another five thousand dollars for not one, but two well-known rock groups, Status Quo and Ozone Zombies. Estimated cost of prom tickets is two hundred dollars per couple."

"Two hundred dollars! She's out of her skull. I know both our classes have been fundraising like crazy all year for this event, but I think we're really stretching the budget as is. And I don't think anyone can afford the cost of those prom tickets. Only Claire's snob friends, and that's because their rich daddies can give them the money," Courtenay said in a disgusted voice.

"That's exactly the point," Delaney said. "I get the feeling that Claire wants to take over this prom and make it her own personal party, with only the kids she deems rich enough and popular enough to be allowed in as guests. In other words, she's deliberately trying to shut all the rest of us out."

"Well, I don't know about that," Helen said in a small voice. She had been nervously playing with her pizza, and now she put it down altogether. "I know you all don't like Claire, or think much of the other girls in the club, but you don't know her like I do. She's really not the scheming snob you seem to think. She means well; she just goes overboard a little."

There were assorted groans and rolled eyes at this

opinion, but no one said anything. Helen inevitably stuck up for the Spirit Club, no matter what anyone else said. As a member, even an invisible and little-liked one, she felt she had to be loyal and defend the members she mistakenly thought were her friends.

"You're calling prom tickets at two hundred dollars a couple a little overboard?" Pammi snorted. "I'd say more like drowning at sea. Good grief, I can't afford to pay those prices, and I can't see many other kids doing it either. But, Delaney, when all is said and done, what can we do about it?"

"Yeah, why get all hot and bothered about something we can't change?" demanded Courtenay.

"Oh, can't we?" asked Delaney in a soft voice. "Can't we?"

All at once, without any warning, an inner ripple of exhilaration surged through Delaney. She had always loved challenges, and bumping up against the Spirit Club looked like it would be the biggest challenge of all. She regarded her friends with a gleam in her eyes. A gleam that hadn't been there before.

"I think we can do something to save the prom *and* show Claire and her 'material girls' a thing or two about romance in the bargain. Now here's my plan . . ."

# Interference from a Bumblebee

*Andrew was terrified. He was hanging onto the edge of the overhead fluorescent lights in English lit for dear life, peering upside down at the class and wondering how he got himself into such a predicament in the first place. A respected young male cupid, swaying high in the air like a tipsy trapeze artist. He hated heights. He hated his bumblebee disguise. But worse than that, he decided, he hated spying on Cupid Delaney.*

*He rolled his eyes around. There she was, sitting in the aisle seat near the window, her curly hair gleaming in the sunlight. Her eyes were focused on the teacher. Her entire face and body radiated absorption and interest. While the clock on the wall inched its way to 9:55, dismissal time, the other kids made bored faces at their friends, collected their books, yawned, and shuffled their feet. Not Cupid Delaney. Mrs. Brandycon read poetry to the class, love poems of Edna St. Vincent Millay, and Cupid Delaney drank in every beautiful line. Her extensive training in the Love Bureau had taught her to appreciate poetry, as well as all the other basic courses taught in high school. Andrew himself loved poetry. Unfortunately, he didn't have the luxury at present of enjoying the words the way he would have liked. In another two minutes the bell would ring. The room would empty. The Monday morning ten o'clock break would occur. And he knew where Cupid Delaney and her friends would be heading. To the Bulletin newspaper office, to implement phase one of the plan. He had to be alert and on his toes (or in this case, his wings) to keep up with Cupid Delaney.*

*It had been a lively weekend for Andrew, perhaps the liveliest he had enjoyed in a long time. Listening in on the plans Cupid Delaney made to fight the Spirit Club, he had gotten as charged up as the girls. And when she had spoken for five minutes on how perfectly romantic and magical attending the right kind of prom could be, using Storm Devrie as an ideal date, the three girls had positively melted. Forget the girls. Andrew had melted. He couldn't help it. Cupid Delaney had to be the most persuasive, stimulating, fun cupid trainee he had ever come across. He loathed his spying tactics. He didn't believe for a moment that this sparkly, self-confident girl would cheat on her promise to Valentina. Why would she have to with such an arsenal of dynamic ammunition all her own: her brains, personality and imagination?*

*9:54 A.M. One more minute left of class. Cupid Delaney never glanced up at the clock. Her eyes were focused in a dreamy haze on Mrs. Brandycon. Across the aisle Alvin Danziger scribbled a note and passed it to her. Andrew could read the words from his high-wire perch overhead: "Good luck with your mission!" Cupid Delaney smiled briefly, then concentrated once more on Edna St. Vincent Millay. Alvin dropped his pencil. As he leaned down to pick it up, his glance fell two rows behind him, where Helen sat. The small, solid-looking girl had been daydreaming and consequently seemed to be staring right into his eyes. Their glances met. Helen blushed, turned away, and dropped her book with a clatter. Alvin hurriedly faced front again, his eyes blinking in embarrassment.*

*Something was going on there, Andrew sensed, observing it*

32

*all. Something registered on his romance pulsars. Maybe neither Alvin nor Helen realized it yet, but there were still definite sparks between them. Trouble ahead, Andrew thought. Because Cupid Delaney had no inkling that an attraction of any kind existed between one of her closest friends and Alvin.*

*The bell rang. Startled, Andrew lost his tenuous grip on the light fixture and plummeted to earth, nearly forgetting to fly in his panic. Bee instincts took over, however, and he glided to safety within the large open tote bag Cupid Delaney carried. Just in time, apparently. With one quick motion, she hurled her bag over her shoulder, collected her books, and hurried out the door where . . .*

. . . an uneasy Helen caught up to Delaney.

"I'm not sure about going through with all this," Helen whispered. "You know, my assignment?"

"Look, Helen, you agreed Saturday night to do it. You said it would be exciting to stand up to the Spirit Club, have them sit up and take notice of you for once."

"I know, I know; it's what they'll do *after* they've noticed me that I'm worried about."

Delaney tossed back her curls. "It's up to you. You're either in with us on Project Dream Prom or not. But if you decide not, that's okay. We won't think any less of you."

Indecision and misgiving gave way to courage. A spark of recklessness glowed in Helen's eyes. "All right, I'm in! Project Dream Prom all the way. Give me the things you want photocopied and I'll have them ready for the noon meeting in Mrs. Argon's office."

"Great!" Delaney dug into her purse, just missing the quivering wing of a large bumblebee that was attached to the zipper section. She pulled out some papers and handed them to Helen. "And don't forget to check with the P.A.

office to stop them from making any further announcements about prom tickets. Tell them to check with Mrs. Argon if anyone questions you. You got that?"

Helen snapped to attention, gave a mock salute. "Yes, ma'am! All orders will be carried out." She started down the hallway, then turned back with a nervous giggle. "I just hope the Spirit Club doesn't do something awful to me!"

"You worry too much," Delaney reassured her. But as she turned to head in the opposite direction, she wondered if she should be worried, too. Dramatic, overbearing Claire Reggio, official head of the Spirit Club and unofficial queen of a large social-climbing contingency in the senior class, was not known for her generous spirit and reservoirs of good will. If Claire wanted something badly enough, like this Power Prom of hers, she'd fight every step of the way to get it. She wouldn't just roll over and play dead and let a few innocuous, previously invisible juniors take the prom away from her. No, this was going to be a challenge, all right, Delaney realized, but one she resolved to win. Not only for herself, to achieve her cupid wings and status, but for the school and especially for her friends in the Saturday Night Dream Club. Pammi, Courtenay, and Helen deserved some real romance in their lives, not the fictitious kind dished up on their favorite soap. Delaney was sure she could help them find dates for the big dance if and when Project Dream Prom was accomplished.

Don't worry about matchmaking now, Delaney thought. Play Scarlett O'Hara and say, "I'll think about it tomorrow. Tomorrow's another day."

Two minutes later she reached the school newspaper office. Impatiently waiting for her outside were Pammi and Courtenay.

34

"Everything going all right?" asked Courtenay by way of greeting.

"So far, so good," Delaney nodded with a grin, "except Helen suffered momentary qualms about participating. But she rallied, and she's having our form copied even as we speak."

"I don't know how you can be so darned chirpy and cheerful at a time like this," Courtenay said. "I'm a nervous wreck."

"You're *always* a nervous wreck," Pammi retorted. "C'mon, lighten up, Wilcox. Project Dream Prom is fun! I'm more excited putting this into operation than watching Storm Devric make love to Tiara Bentley on 'Young Dreamers.' "

"Then you're really in trouble, girl," Courtenay said. "It's time you asked your mother about the birds and the bees."

"Ha, ha. Seriously, Court, aren't you enjoying it at all—the secret weekend meetings, the code words, the feeling of power in upsetting the Spirit Club?"

Courtenay looked at her friend in surprise. "Of *course* I'm enjoying it. I just enjoy it better if I can worry about it, too."

Pammi and Delaney exchanged glances and laughed.

"All right," Delaney said, "first order of business. Courtenay, I want you to go to the music department and then the student lounge if you have time and start drumming up volunteers for tomorrow. Get all your friends in the orchestra and pep band excited. Tell them they'll be needed outside school tomorrow morning at seven-forty-five sharp. Instructions will be issued at that time."

"My word, she's not only chirpy and cheerful, but she's confident, too," Courtenay moaned. "You're talking as if I can snap my fingers and have hundreds of friends do my bidding."

"Well, can't you? Go on, give it your best shot. You've got ten minutes to produce a miracle."

Courtenay looked at Delaney as if she wanted to say something negative, but decided against it. "Music department first. Wonder Woman Wilcox is on her way."

"Oh, and Court? Remember, twelve sharp in Mrs. Argon's room today. We mustn't keep Claire and the Spirit Club waiting."

"Heaven forbid." With a grin and a wave, Courtenay hurried off.

"Of course the thought never crossed your mind that Mitch usually takes his breaks in the music department, practicing with his group?" Pammi asked lightly.

"All the more reason for Courtenay to be there. If Muhammad doesn't come to the mountain, then the mountain can come to the music department. And let the sparks fly, if there are any. Personally, despite Court's denials, I think there are some."

"You don't need to convince me, remember? I'm the one who always tries to get her to show Mitch her music cassettes. She's really talented, but she's too scared to open up and let other people know. Speaking of secrets, deep, dark secrets," Pammi continued, "Claire doesn't know what the noon meeting's about, right? She's still in the dark?"

Delaney nodded. "When I talked to Mrs. Argon before school, she promised she wouldn't say a word as to why she asked the Spirit Club to meet in her office today. Just some matters to do with the prom. She's the senior advisor supervising the prom planning committee, so Claire can't be suspicious. Claire and Beth and Wendy and Dawn know nothing about our little surprise, I guarantee. So sorry, Ms. Reggio. I think your little egotistical balloon will burst, like your Mogul Madness prom, this very Monday. But we have work to do ourselves." Delaney gazed up and down the hall as if searching for enemy agents. She lowered her voice. "Operation SNAP."

"Operation SNAP! Snatch the Article about the Prom. I love it! I really do! What a clever title!"

"That's because you thought of it, remember?"

"I always think of the good things; that's what makes me undisputed class clown," Pammi plowed on. "But seriously, Delaney, we can't get caught. I'd lose my job on the paper, and I'd hate that. You know I want to be features editor next year."

"I promised we'd be careful, and we will. When we go inside, I'll divert attention while you poke through the In box for any articles about the prom. I'm sure Beth Simpson or Claire persuaded Tim to print something about it. And it's just Claire's style, too. Entice all the kids, show off about the glamorous, extravagant evening she's organizing, but then hit them with the fact that it's too expensive to attend and eat your hearts out, please."

"I don't understand her."

"Be happy. It means you're a healthy, sensitive human being. Now let's go—"

But Pammi's hand shot out and gripped her arm. Her voice dwindled to a squeak. "Speaking of sensitive human beings, look who's heading our way! The Bratt!"

"Relax, Pammi. And quit trying to choke my arm to death. Thank you. Duck in the *Bulletin* office with me, and maybe he won't see us. He might not be coming in here at all."

"Not coming in here? The overlord practically camps out here. Every chance he gets he haunts this place and browbeats all the poor serfs who write copy for him."

*37*

"Come on!"

Delaney yanked Pammi inside the cramped room that served as the *Bulletin*'s headquarters. Formerly a maintenance supply room, it now boasted the latest in word processing equipment and a state-of-the-art printer, as well as several antiquated filing cabinets and small odd-sized tables that doubled as desks and chairs. Only one person was in the office, a sharp-faced girl working at the computer.

"Oh, great," Pammi whispered. "Suzi Ramos, the Bratt's henchwoman. She's the assistant editor and his biggest fan. Change of plans! I'll do the fast talking while you get to work on snooping. Try the green In box on the desk by the wall."

"What are you doing here?" Suzi turned a disbelieving face to Pammi. "You never come to the office unless Tim orders you to. You're always complaining about getting claustrophobia in here."

"Change of heart, I guess," Pammi quipped. She stood in front of Suzi to block the sight of Delaney feverishly pawing through the files.

"Change of heart, that's rich. And what's that girl doing back there?"

Before Pammi could think of a reasonable answer, Timothy Bratt walked into the room. He was wearing a perfectly starched madras shirt and perfectly creased khaki pants; even his slicked-back brown hair looked ironed and perfectly in place. For once, both Delaney and Pammi were happy to see him. Suzi forgot her suspicions to question him about staff matters. But he waved her off to stare at Pammi.

"Where's the piece on the freshman auction? It's due today."

"Freshman auction . . ." Pammi pretended to think,

stretching her arms in the air in order to give Delaney more coverage and more time to locate the article. "Why, I thought I turned that piece in. Friday, as a matter of fact. And I gave it to Suzi."

"Well, I never saw it!" Suzi sputtered in indignation. "I'm sure I never received it or I would have put it on Timothy's desk."

"And I never saw it," Tim said.

"Maybe you missed it," Pammi suggested airily. "In all that clutter . . ."

"There's no clutter on Timothy's desk!" Suzi protested.

"That's right, I forgot." Pammi grinned. "He organizes and files everything so perfectly. Even his garbage. Why don't we check the round file and look under *D*, for debris?"

While Suzi protested and Tim's blue-eyed stare turned frosty, Delaney inwardly groaned behind them. Pammi was doing it again. She was making fun of Tim Bratt because she was nervous around him. And he couldn't tell that she liked him beneath all that sarcasm. Forget playing cupid for one minute and concentrate, Delaney chastised herself. Try to find the article. She scrabbled wildly in the green box as Suzi said, "The story on the prom is nearly finished. I'm just entering it on the computer now."

Both Pammi and Delaney gasped at the same time. Tim wheeled around and spotted Delaney.

"Who the heck are you and what are you doing in the office?"

Caught with her hand in the cookie jar, or in this case, the In box, Delaney straightened and tried to smile innocently at the forbidding-looking boy and suspicious assistant editor.

"Why, uh, I'm friends with Pammi and she's told me so many wonderful things about you (Pammi glared at this but Delaney swept right on), about working at the *Bulletin*, that I thought I'd visit the office and get a feel for journalism. You know, see if I'd like working here next year."

Tim's face had softened under Delaney's angelic smile, but Suzi still looked suspicious.

"That doesn't explain why you were going through private material," Suzi said, "and I think—"

Before they could learn what Suzi thought, a very fat and frightening looking bumblebee rumbled into view and landed on her computer. Suzi shrieked, jumped up, and then crashed her fingers down on the console. Strange combinations of letters appeared on the screen.

"The article! We've lost the article!" Suzi cried.

"Forget the article. It's the computer I'm worried about," Tim barked.

All four of them stared at the flashing, beeping computer. Two of those watching privately turned cartwheels inside. No one noticed that the catalyst in this matter had silently crawled underneath a desk and was peering out at the chaos in great good humor.

"Wait a sec; something's come up on the printer."

Tim, Pammi, and Delaney joined Suzi and watched sheet after sheet roll out with the letters "BzzzzBzzzz-Bzzzz."

"Saved by the bzzzz," Delaney murmured to Pammi.

Would she be so lucky with the Spirit Club this afternoon?

40

# The Brainstorm

At precisely five minutes to noon Delaney arrived at Mrs. Argon's office and stood outside the door. The hallway was crowded with laughing, shouting kids on their lunch break, but Delaney didn't notice them. She kept thinking about Alvin and their brief conversation after fourth-period history.

He had rushed up to her in the hallway, his face beaming, the glasses slipping down his nose in excitement.

"Delaney, you'll never guess what just happened! Mr. Dawkings approved my idea for an Environment Now club at school. And guess who he wants to head it? Me!"

"Oh, Alvin, that's fantastic!" Delaney cried, knowing only too well how much the formation of this organization meant to Alvin. But his next words caught her off-guard and dampened her enthusiasm.

"If I'm going to be president, then my first order of business will be to appoint my vice-president. And I can't think of anyone better than you, Delaney!"

"Me!"

"Of course, you! You'd be perfect! You're as concerned and as interested in preserving our planet as anyone else I know. And you're a terrific organizer. With your outgoing personality and great ideas, I bet we get a lot of kids to sign up. Senior year we'll be closer than ever!"

"Senior year . . ."

"Yes, senior year. Ring a bell? The one that follows junior year? Is there some problem I don't know about?"

She thought quickly, hands twisting together in anxiety. A problem? Oh, there was a problem all right. How could she possibly tell Alvin that she would not be able to help him organize his club next year because next year she would not be attending Woodside High? Next year she would be enrolled in the Love Bureau, busy with her cupid responsibilities. In less than two weeks she would disappear completely from Alvin's life, and he would never see her again. Delaney stared into the animated face of this special boy, and her heart sank. All at once she realized how lonely Alvin would be without her. She'd have her cupid wings and her cupid world to soften the pain of separation, but Alvin would have nothing. How could she have failed to understand this when Valentina assigned her the mission? How could she have been so selfish?

Somehow she had managed to slip away from Alvin without lying to him or making him too suspicious, but the time would come, very soon, when she'd have to deal with the problem. There must be something she could do for Alvin. But what? No easy answer sprang to mind.

The twelve o'clock bell rang, breaking into her gloomy thoughts. Time for action and the prom committee meeting. She just wished her spirits were livelier, her mood happier. Thinking about Alvin made her feel depressed and unequal to locking horns with Claire Reggio. With a sinking feeling in the pit of her stomach, Delaney began to open the door when Trip Hawkins, Woodside's resident bad boy and detention king, roared down the hall on his motorcycle. Kids scattered and dropped their books. The motorcycle was charging right at her, apparently out of control, when someone grabbed her arm and pushed her out of danger against the lockers. Trip went careening on past and ended up in the assistant principal's outer office as an apt finale.

"Great Venus, he almost hit me!" Delaney gasped, but then was more frightened that she had actually used a Love Bureau expression in public than by her near miss. How could she have let that slip? But her rescuer didn't change expression or blink an eye. In fact, Delaney changed expression and blinked *her* eyes when she saw who had rescued her.

He was a tall, golden-haired boy she had never seen before, yet whose features seemed oddly familiar. He had attractively colored eyes that were a black-flecked golden, like a lion's, and were warm and admiring as he stared down at her. The boy had even features, the kind of body you see in body-building magazines or on a pedestal in a museum, and an oddly vulnerable smile. He was wearing a lemony yellow- and black-striped pullover and black cords, and he almost *hummed* with a kind of restless energy. He was absolutely gorgeous, a fifteen on a scale of one to ten, and why hadn't she ever noticed him before at school? How could he keep those blazing blond looks quiet?

"Are you all right?" The concern in his eyes was real.

"I'm—I'm fine." Why did she have this uncontrollable urge to blurt out her troubles and fears to this boy, this total stranger who somehow didn't seem like a stranger at all? She was nervous, heart racing wildly, and that wasn't like her.

"Everything's going to be okay," he said in a gentle voice. But he didn't seem to be reassuring her about the motorcycle scare as much as the upcoming meeting with the Spirit Club. He tapped a playful finger on her nose.

And suddenly at this touch she felt her entire mood change. She felt on top of the world, raring to go, as confident and as cheerful as ever. Chirpy is what Courtenay called it. Look out, Spirit Club. Move over, Claire Reggio. A new force is in town and it's called Cupid Delaney and she packs a mean Dream Prom.

A group of girls giggling and racing down the hall bumped into Delaney and her newfound friend, and she dropped her books. She bent to pick them up, and he was gone. Vanished. Disappeared in an instant in the swirling mass of kids.

"Hey, wait a minute!" she cried, searching for the gleaming gold head in the crowd. "I didn't get a chance to thank you . . ."

Or ask your name, she thought. Funny how his features looked vaguely familiar.

Pammi and Courtenay hurried toward her.

"Did you see him? Did you see him?" Delaney exploded.

"Whoa, slow down," Pammi said. "See who?"

"A tall blond guy, all sunshiny and humming, with a yellow and black shirt . . ."

"Sunshiny? Humming?" Pammi exchanged glances with Courtenay. "Is she putting us on or what?"

Delaney's face fell. "That's strange. He was standing right here—oh, well, never mind. We have more important things to worry about. Like this meeting with the Spirit Club. But you know something, girls? I'm not worried at all. Not one tiny bit. So full steam ahead. The Queen of Woodside High awaits us."

The three of them giggled nervously, then put on solemn faces as they filed into Mrs. Argon's office. But the Queen of Woodside High did not await anyone there. Claire Reggio was absent. Delaney had to wonder if the head of the Drama Club wanted to make a late entrance for effect.

The rest of her group was sitting on chairs and one of the two large sofas arranged in a semicircle for the meeting. They began whispering when Delaney, Pammi, and Courtenay walked in. Obviously they had no idea what to expect.

Mrs. Argon sat off to one side of her desk, wisps of brown hair escaping her bun. She greeted Delaney, who introduced her to Pammi and Courtenay.

"Do the rest of you know one another? Want to go around the room and introduce yourselves?" she suggested.

"Shouldn't we wait for Claire?" one of the girls asked.

"If we wait for Claire, we may be here until graduation night," Pammi muttered. Dawn Cummings, one of Claire's best friends, overheard the remark and frowned. Pammi smiled sweetly.

Delaney, Pammi, and Courtenay sank onto the empty sofa. They found themselves staring directly across the room at nine members of the Spirit Club, including a visibly nervous Helen, who was chewing on the eraser tip of a pencil.

"Well, for Pete's sake, why is Helen sitting in their camp?" Pammi whispered to Delaney. "It doesn't look right."

Delaney smiled at Helen, but Helen could only manage a quirk of one lip before compulsively nibbling the pencil. "Poor kid, she's terrified. Just as long as she votes with us, though, it doesn't matter where she sits."

"*If* she votes with us, you mean," Courtenay interjected.

"Don't be such a pessimist," Pammi said.

Delaney fished in her large tote bag and produced a file folder. "She copied our Dream Prom flyers and ballots, so I'm sure she's with us. Anyway, we'll have to persuade a few more people than Helen to vote our way as well. But I don't see any problems once they hear our theme."

"You sure are cocky today," Pammi whispered. "Don't see any problems? I see eight of them at this very moment, and they're glaring at us and wondering why they've been dragged away from their lunch."

"They'll find out as soon as Claire gets here."

Delaney thumbed through the flyers with a proud smile, then sat back. Confidently she glanced over at the members of the Spirit Club. There were Dawn Cummings and Wendy Chu, varsity cheerleaders and student council members; Beth Simpson, sweet-faced but acid-tongued secretary of the senior class. Poor Helen had been no match for the female contingent of the Spirit Club with their gossipy ways and superficial interests in shopping and fashion. But somehow, in her own tenacious way, the stubborn junior had stuck it out.

Delaney next turned her attention to the five boys: Craig Lacrosse and Tom Delacruz, good friends and big jocks at school, the party animals. They'd definitely be under Claire's thumb and never question a word she said. Then there was Tim Bratt, *Bulletin* editor and head of the debate team, and his counterpart on the yearbook, John Howards, a short, plump guy noted for a dark sense of humor. They were definitely movers and shakers in the school, but they also seemed to think for themselves. Last but not least, there was Mitch Rhyner. He was a question mark, but a darkly attractive one.

Mitch was of medium height, stocky, with long, dark hair curling around his shoulders. He had sleepy eyes and a drop-dead voice that made him Woodside High's pick for future rock fame. Right now he performed less exciting jobs like heading the Service Commission and coaching the frosh baseball team. He sprawled easily on the floor, long legs encased in cowboy boots, and met Delaney's speculative gaze with a wink.

Down, girl, Delaney thought. You're not the one he's really watching out of the corner of those outrageously sexy eyes. It's Courtenay. And she keeps frowning and peeking at him and peeking at him and frowning. If she'd smile at him just once, show him the least bit of encouragement . . .

The same with Pammi and Tim. They were sitting across from each other and taking great pains to pretend how involved they were in talking to their friends. But their eyes kept shifting back and forth like windshield wipers on a rainy night. All this potential for love and romance made Delaney even more determined to succeed in her mission. Woodside High would have the most spectacular Dream Prom imaginable.

The door was flung open, and Claire Reggio rushed into the room with the dramatic force of a whirlwind. More like a tornado, Delaney thought, watching Claire shower apologies left and right and then shuffle people around to secure the most comfortable seat in the room for herself. The air became charged with a tension that hadn't been there before. It focused entirely on the newly arrived president of the Spirit Club. Claire looked like a model for a designer jeans ad, with masses of black curly hair that tumbled past her shoulders, glittering emerald eyes outlined in purple and green, and a pouty mouth so red it could have stopped traffic at an intersection. She wore men's clothes—an oversized white shirt, baggy trousers with suspenders, and to top it off, her trademark, a fedora hat. Dressed in such a masculine style, Claire emphasized her femininity. It was a clever way to stand out, and no one did it better, Delaney had to admit.

Claire immediately took over.

"What's the reason behind this meeting, Mrs. Argon? I've got a play to rehearse for the senior talent show, and I don't have a minute to spare."

"And of course we little peons do?" said Pammi. She rolled her eyes at Delaney.

Claire heard the remark and seemed to notice the three girls for the first time. Her eyes narrowed.

"Who are these students and why are they at a closed meeting of the Spirit Club?"

Mrs. Argon smiled. "Let's start off by going around the room and introducing ourselves, and then I'll explain."

"But—"

"Introductions," said Mrs. Argon firmly.

Claire pouted and then proceeded to rattle off her name too quickly to be understood. The girls in the Spirit Club laughed and imitated Claire. Like mindless puppets, Delaney thought. Whatever Claire did or said, no matter how silly or childish, they copied. When introductions were over, Mrs. Argon spoke up.

"First, to clarify something, this is not a Spirit Club meeting. This is a prom committee meeting."

"But the Spirit Club's running the prom," Claire said.

"This is what the meeting's about. To discuss the junior/senior prom and who can work on it. Now, whether you realized it or not, the prom committee is open to any member of the junior or senior class who wants to volunteer. And these three girls, Delaney, Courtenay, and Pammi, want to volunteer their time and energy to help you. I'm sure you'll be pleased that they want to participate, and what's even better, they're all juniors, so you'll be able to get more input from the junior class."

Claire stiffened. The set to her jaw became pronounced. "Input from more juniors? I'm sure you meant well, but the seniors in the Spirit Club have the planning of the prom well under control, and we don't need any help. And I cannot believe there's any such ruling or school policy that allows, well, just *anyone* to waltz in and work on such an important social event as the junior/senior prom."

*Just anyone*, Delaney repeated to herself. No, Ms. Snob Reggio, we're not just anyone. And you're going to find that out soon enough.

Barely managing to keep a straight face, Delaney opened the folder on her lap and pulled out a piece of paper.

"If I may introduce something? A copy of page one hundred and ten from the *Woodside High School Rules and Regulations Handbook*, stating in section six that all students who wish to volunteer with organizing the junior/senior prom will be automatically elected to the prom committee and cannot be excluded due to any class or personality conflicts." Delaney looked directly across at Claire. "Should I give this to your secretary to copy for the minutes?"

At first it seemed that Claire was going to lash out at her in a childish display of temper, but she controlled herself. She made a dismissive hand movement, as if recording something so trivial was beneath the dignity of the Spirit Club.

"Don't bother. I'm sure the archaic rules must be correct. Helen, please add this to your notes: The Spirit Club graciously welcomed three new members to the prom committee—and get the spelling of their names right. You've been making a few too many errors in your grammar and spelling lately."

Claire's face was smooth and haughty again. Delaney suspected that Claire had agreed to include the juniors to placate Mrs. Argon, but that she fully intended to continue her dictatorship exactly as before, with the Spirit Club as a massive steamroller flattening out any opposition.

Claire looked at her watch and made a motion to rise. "Well, if that's all . . ."

"Not quite all," Mrs. Argon said. Claire frowned and sat back down. "Delaney?"

"Sock it to her," Pammi whispered.

Delaney allowed herself a small private smile before beginning. Ten minutes ago, outside Mrs. Argon's office, she had been a miserable, self-doubting wreck, but a chance encounter with an unusual boy had changed all that. She felt alive with confidence and exhilaration, eager to share her theme of a Dream Prom with the Spirit Club.

Outside the slightly opened window, a bumblebee buzzed back and forth. It slipped inside the room and landed on Mrs. Argon's desk, taking refuge behind a half-eaten container of yogurt. No one noticed the humming intruder. All eyes were fixed on Delaney.

"I want to introduce a theme for the prom," she began, but got no further as Claire cut her off.

"We have a theme."

"And it's perfect," added Dawn. Dawn and Claire exchanged self-satisfied smiles.

"May I at least present my idea?" asked Delaney. "It's called a Dream Prom, and I've typed up a sample ballot that lists the song, colors, motto, and flower that illustrate the theme."

Pammi handed out the red flyers. Claire accepted hers as if it were a decaying fish and began reading it aloud in a smug voice.

"Let's see, Dream Prom as theme. How quaint. But better than Beach Blanket Under the Stars or A Night to Remember. Colors: red and white. Red and white?" She wrinkled her nose. "Snow on a fire hydrant?"

"Lace on a valentine," Mitch suggested with a grin at Courtenay. Courtenay frowned and looked away. "Or a red carnation on a white satin dress. It's got possibilities for a song."

"Well, don't let the muse carry you away just yet," Claire snapped. "There's more to a prom than poetic colors."

"So glad you see they're poetic," Delaney said with a deadpan face. "Maybe you'll think the same about the other items."

Almost grinding her teeth, Claire continued reading. "Song: 'Dream Only of Me.' "

"Ooh, I *love* that song!" cried Wendy, forgetting whose side she was on. "And Storm Devrie! To die for."

Claire shot Wendy a forbidding look, and Wendy instantly subsided.

"Flower," Claire continued, "red rose. Appropriate, but maybe a little too corny? Motto: 'Lead with the heart.' "

Beth and Dawn broke into subdued snickers that were immediately squelched when Tim asked, "Well, what was our motto? You never did let the guys in on any of the prom decisions."

"What did you decide, Claire?" Delaney asked innocently. "I'm sure we all want to know."

Claire hesitated, then said, " 'Reach for the stars . . . and carry a platinum American Express card.' For a Mogul Madness theme."

"What!" Tim sat up in horror.

"We had a second choice of 'High on life, bullish on the stock market,' " added Wendy.

51

"Something's bullish, all right," pronounced an astonished Mitch. " 'Lead with the heart' sounds a lot better to me."

"Me, too," said Tim.

"Don't be so trite and conventional," Claire said in a strained voice. "Every single prom in every single high school in the nation will have gushy, mushy, moon, June, love themes. Let's be different. Be creative. Show the other schools how old-fashioned and out of style they are."

"I agree," Craig said.

"Me, too," Tom added.

All around the room heads were beginning to bob to the dominating tune Claire Reggio played. Delaney's high spirits started to droop. It couldn't be going poorly. It just couldn't. Had she been daydreaming before about the successful outcome of this all-important meeting?

"I'm so sorry, Delaney," Claire said in a distinctly nonapologetic voice. "You obviously meant well, but our theme prevails."

"Does it?" inquired Tim. "I think we should take a vote."

"A vote!" The dark-haired girl turned a disbelieving face toward Tim.

"Yes, Claire, a vote. Don't make it sound like a four-letter word. As I recall, you never let the male half of the Spirit Club have any say in the prom, and fair is fair. We're members and we deserve to be heard."

"Everyone should be heard and everyone should vote," corrected Mrs. Argon. "Remember, this is not the Spirit Club; it's the prom committee, of which these three girls are now official members. Now, you all know Claire's theme, and you have Delaney's ballot in front of you. Will it be Mogul Madness or Dream Prom? Let's see a show of hands. First, how many in favor of the Dream Prom?"

Before anyone had time to raise a hand, Delaney thought fast and furiously. An inner voice tempted her. Use your powers and make them vote the way you want them to. It's as simple as a three-word incantation. You're going to fail your assignment if you don't, the devilish voice persisted. Hurry, make everyone decide to cast his or her vote for the Dream Prom. Do it now.

*At the very moment Delaney rejected using her powers, someone else decided to use them for her. Andrew crawled out from behind the yogurt container, determined to help Cupid Delaney. If he got into trouble for it, so be it. It would be worth it to see the blonde girl smile and regain her optimism.*

*"All right, don't be shy," Mrs. Argon prompted. "Show of hands for the Dream Prom." The senior advisor fumbled on her cluttered desk for her glasses and pushed a stack of books directly in front of Andrew. It towered over him like the Washington Monument. He couldn't see a thing, could only hear the voting take place. How many were supporting Cupid Delaney at this crucial moment? There was only one way to find out. Wedged in among all the objects on the desk, he couldn't fly, so he rapidly scaled the yogurt container. The sight that greeted his eyes from this vantage point startled him. Six out of the thirteen present were voting in favor of Cupid Delaney's theme. Mrs. Argon scribbled their names on a clipboard: "Delaney, Pammi, Courtenay, Tim, Mitch, John . . . six votes. Anyone else?"*

*It seemed to Andrew that all eyes in the room were directed at Helen. If she voted for the Dream Prom, Mogul Madness would only be a bad memory. But Helen's face was stiff and expressionless. Andrew realized she wasn't strong enough to stand up to Claire and the Spirit Club. So he had to be strong and stand up for her and persuade her in true Love Bureau fashion.*

*As Mrs. Argon called, "Anyone else?", Andrew prepared to fly. His back leg was caught, however, on the rim of the container, and as he tried to free himself, he lost his balance and toppled backward into the gooey mounds of strawberry-flavored yogurt.*

*It was too late. Too late to do anything. He had failed Cupid Delaney. Andrew twitched helplessly and angrily in his sticky, sweet prison as . . .*

. . . Delaney realized that she had lost to Claire Reggio. The dark-haired girl shot a smug smile across the room at her as Mrs. Argon said, "All right, those in favor of Mogul Madness?"

Again, six hands went up. Mrs. Argon called off the names: "Claire, Tom, Beth, Wendy, Dawn, Craig . . ."

Delaney looked at Helen, huddled miserably in her chair. Poor Helen. Delaney could well imagine what her friend was going through.

"Helen," Claire said, manicured hand high in the air, "we're waiting."

There was a pause.

"Helen . . . ?" Claire's icy tone conveyed a threat.

Another pause, and then Helen's face lightened. "I'm abstaining."

Claire and her friends gasped.

"She can't abstain!" Dawn cried.

"Yes, she can, and she has," Mrs. Argon said. "It's perfectly legal to abstain. So that makes our voting a tie. What do we do about it? Any suggestions?"

Claire drew herself up. "If you think we'll flip a coin or draw straws, well . . ."

Delaney's heart had stopped, and now it beat normally again. Maybe Fate or Fortune was smiling down at her after all. Or the chance encounter with the unknown boy had brought her luck. Whatever—she'd make the most out of the miracle. The success of the mission was still in her grasp.

"I have an idea," Delaney said.

The gleam was back in her eyes.

# The Dream Team Kicks Off

It had been a miracle. Delaney's idea had worked. Idea? More like dream scheme, she thought. A Dream Scheme for a Dream Prom.

After the tie vote in the newly reorganized prom committee Monday, Delaney had suggested letting the entire junior and senior classes have a voice in the matter and decide which of the two themes they preferred. Claire had made a face, tapping those fire-engine-red fingernails in barely suppressed fury on the arm of the sofa, but Mrs. Argon had liked the idea. And Tim, John, and Mitch had sided with Delaney and overruled the objections of the irritated Spirit Club members.

Delaney and her friends and Claire and her loyal Spirit Club followers would both have three days in which to "tell and sell" the school on their respective prom themes. On Friday morning the junior and senior classes would cast their ballots for either a romantic dream dance or a fast-track power prom.

Delaney hoped, for her own sake, for the sake of her cupid mission, and for the sake of the school, that the hearts and flowers theme would win. She'd be in big trouble if she lost. And she hated to disappoint the Love

Bureau and the Great Love Goddess herself. How shattering to imagine love and romance becoming passé among teenagers. If girls like Claire Reggio and Dawn Cummings had their way, it might. But not if Delaney could help it. She had stayed after school Monday to recruit all the volunteers she could, and now, bright and early Tuesday morning, a half hour before the first bell rang, she was ready to roll up her sleeves and go to work.

This is fun, she suddenly thought, watching her small group of friends assemble at the front entrance of Woodside. It's fun and exciting because I don't know what's going to happen over the next three days, and as a cupid trainee, I'd always know. Using Love Bureau powers guarantees a predictable outcome. But not using powers means risk taking, uncertainty, and unpredictability. It also means adventure—especially with a committee of kids this size. It's not exactly the mob scene in *The Hunchback of Notre Dame*, Delaney thought, but it's a start.

"All right, gather round," she instructed from her position on the top step. "I want to go over assignments."

Tim Bratt, Suzi Ramos, John Howards, Alvin, and several other kids edged closer to Delaney.

Pammi tried to stifle a yawn and failed. "She's talking assignments and it's seven-thirty in the morning, for pity's sake. I'm still not awake yet. Here, Court, give me a hand. When our captain calls, we must obey."

Pammi staggered under the weight of a heavy, rolled-up banner and with Courtenay's assistance, managed to bring it to the front steps.

"Court and I were up last night past midnight working on this blasted banner," Pammi said with a scowl. "So you'd better appreciate it. We even had my dad and mom on their hands and knees, wielding a mean paintbrush."

"I'm sure it's great," Delaney assured her. "Let's see it."

"If you can paint even half as well as you write, it's got to be a winner," Tim offered.

Pammi flashed him a suspicious look, but his compliment seemed genuine. Flustered, she helped Courtenay unroll the six-foot-long sign. Cries of approval met their handiwork. Bordered in lines of pink and red and adorned with hearts and roses, huge Gothic-style letters spelled out *Dream Prom*. Running vertically beneath the individual letters of *Prom* were the words *Put Romance on the Menu*.

"Fantastic!" cried John. "We should take a picture for the yearbook."

"For the *Bulletin*, too," agreed Tim. For once, his always serious features were animated. "Suzi, where's the camera?"

Pammi jumped up and down. "This is so great. Think of all the publicity we'll get! The paper comes out Thursday, which should be perfect. Talk about free advertising!"

"But is it fair?" Suzi asked, reluctantly pulling out the school camera. "I mean, won't Claire make a fuss because we seem to be endorsing the Dream Prom? The *Bulletin* is supposed to be unbiased."

Tim hesitated. "Well . . ."

"Why not run the photograph in the activities-about-school column?" Pammi improvised quickly. She snapped her fingers. "Or better yet, let someone do a feature article about the whole prom question. It's certainly an issue and worth a spread in the paper. I happen to know the perfect writer to cover the story, too."

"Three guesses as to the perfect writer's identity," Suzi injected sourly. "But there's only one problem. We've already laid out the copy for Thursday's edition."

"So we change it," Tim said. "I like Pammi's idea."

"Well, this is a first," Pammi cried. "Timothy Bratt actually taking an idea from one of his staff members and using it. Why, I—"

Delaney hurriedly raised a hand to cut Pammi off. Any more sarcasm and the extraordinary détente between Tim and Pammi would refreeze into their usual cold war. "Sorry to interrupt, but you two can work on *Bulletin* business on your own time. Right now we need to choose assignments and get the banner up."

"Are we allowed to put signs over the entrance?" one of the girls asked.

Delaney nodded. "I got permission from the vice-principal herself. We can hang the banner this morning, but it comes down right after the second bell. It doesn't matter, though. Just seeing what it says and then having volunteers hand out flyers and ballots by the entrance will make kids aware that something's going on about the prom and that they have a say in the matter. It's just to wake them up."

"I wish I could wake up," Pammi grumbled. "I hop you don't expect us to get here this bright and early ever morning."

"Until Friday I do," Delaney said. "That's part of tl plan. We keep advertising and selling our theme to t juniors and seniors until they're so worn down they ju have to vote for our idea."

She turned to Alvin, who wore an I-wish-I-could-anywhere-but-here expression on his face. Delaney ognized the look. She knew the red-haired boy di really like getting involved in social activities at Wood and was only present this morning to show Delane cared. Well, she cared about Alvin, and that was why wanted to create the most magical night for Woo

High's prom. This would be her only prom. She wanted to make it a perfect last date with Alvin.

"Alvin, could you hunt up Mr. Grabble or any of the other maintenance staff and find a ladder? We need to hang the banner before the kids start arriving."

Always eager to help, Alvin nodded and loped away. Delaney watched him go with a sigh. She would really miss him. Then she produced a stack of bright red flyers and a list from her shoulder bag. "All right, assignment time. Everyone ready?"

"Ready and waiting," Courtenay said with a smile. "Let's do it!"

Pammi turned an astonished eye on her friend. "Why, Courtenay Wilcox, did my ears deceive me, or was that a positive statement I heard escaping from those perennially pessimistic lips of yours?"

"Positive. Guilty as charged." Courtenay tossed her chin-length hair back.

"Does this newfound positive attitude have anything at all to do with someone we know? Someone who's medium tall, very dark and sexy? And speaking of the mighty M.R., where is he? I thought he wanted to help."

Courtenay gave a studied shrug of indifference. "I'm sure I don't know. Mitch Rhyner is his own person. He doesn't confide in me. And I'm glad," she hastily added, although her cheeks were turning pink. "He was probably mobbed on his way over here by a bunch of overzealous groupies."

"Helen isn't here either," Pammi whispered.

"Do you blame her?" Courtenay sniffed. "After yesterday's scene in Mrs. Argon's office, she probably feels too embarrassed to show her face. Imagine, siding with Claire against us, her own friends!"

"She didn't side with Claire; she abstained," Delaney

said. "And that took courage. By not actually voting for Claire's prom idea, she was voting against it. And it may jeopardize her standing in the Spirit Club."

"Would that be so terrible?" Pammi asked.

"For Helen it would. Now can we get back to business— oh. Here comes Mr. Grabble and Alvin with the ladder. Good." She told them where she wanted the sign placed and then continued. "I need volunteers this morning to greet kids and hand out these prom flyers. As you give them a flyer, be sure to tell them they have a voice in choosing the theme and that voting's on Friday morning. And don't forget to mention the rally after school on Thursday. It's all written on the flyer."

Several kids stepped forward.

"Remember," she urged, passing out flyers, "be enthusiastic. Be spirited. Attitude is everything."

"I'll have to jot down that motto when I take my SATs," Courtenay groaned. She stepped forward to volunteer.

"I need someone to put flyers and ballots on the bulletin board and on all the windshields of the cars in the parking lot. Also on the activities wall; everywhere you see a blank space, slap one of these flyers up."

More volunteers stepped forward. Ballots were passed out.

"I've got announcements for the P.A. system. Who wants to be a movie star and deliver them over the air?"

John Howards grinned sheepishly and nodded. Delaney gave him the notice. Then she stepped back to observe the final placement of the banner.

"That's fantastic," she declared. "Even better and more eye-catching than I envisioned. The kids will stop dead in their tracks when they see it this morning. They can't fail to. And *Put Romance On the Menu* for the letters in *Prom* is clever."

"That's me," Pammi grinned. "Clever."

"And oh so modest," Courtenay added with a laugh. She squinted up at the banner. "But seriously, does the sign really look okay?"

"What did I tell you before? Think positive, girl," Pammi said.

And then, swinging up the circular driveway to the school, came a honking parade of cars, with a shiny blue flatbed truck in the lead. In the back of the truck sat a group of laughing guys in Service Commission caps and jackets, clutching red and white balloons. With a squeal of brakes, the cars came to a stop. The guys jumped out of the truck, and all the other kids spilled out of the cars.

"Don't look now, but it's the whole Service Commission and what looks like the entire pep band," said Courtenay. "I talked to them yesterday during the morning break, but I never thought they'd actually show up to help. They seemed so lackluster about the prom this year. I don't understand what changed their minds . . ."

Her voice trailed off when she saw who leaped out of the driver's side of the truck and strode over to the steps.

"Now do you understand the big turnout?" Pammi murmured. "It's spelled Mitch Rhyner, and it's wonderful."

Mitch hooked his fingers into his jeans pockets and slanted a devilish grin at Courtenay. "Are these the volunteers you wanted?"

As Courtenay couldn't seem to make a sound, but stood there with her mouth open in surprise, Delaney took over.

"This is great! We need all the volunteers we can get! And the balloons! I can't believe it. Where did you get them?"

Mitch beckoned one of his friends who was holding a balloon over and handed the balloon to Delaney with a small bow. "Compliments of my uncle's flower store. Uncle Sid seems to think that donating these balloons to your cause might give you the idea of sponsoring his shop for corsages for the prom."

"Uncle Sid's got a point," Delaney said. She held up the bouncy helium balloon and laughed. Shiny white and red, it depicted a dewy-eyed Miss Piggy puckered up for a kiss from an equally starry-eyed Kermit the Frog. "If the Dream Prom wins, I'll be sure to give his flower store publicity and advertising. These are so great, Kermit kissing Miss Piggy."

"And the balloons go with the theme," Pammi said. "Love Is in the Air. Or, High on Love."

A few kids groaned, but Delaney nodded. "Why not? It's funny! Listen, Mitch, can we get some of your volunteers to attach the balloons to the banner somehow, maybe a group of balloons on either side? And maybe tie some into the ivy by the door?"

"No problem." Mitch rattled off names, kids jumped into action, and seconds later the front entrance was a beehive of activity. A large bumblebee perched on the top edge of the banner, humming cheerfully and nervously retreating behind the sign when several boys climbed up the ladder to position the balloons. The bee poked one eye out and continued to observe it all.

Down below, Mitch directed his volunteers to clear the driveway, himself in the lead, and the procession of cars headed for the school parking lot with horns honking and radios blaring. Moments later kids reappeared carrying clarinets, trombones, flutes, and even one large drum.

"Gotta have music to sell a theme," Mitch explained. "What'll it be, Miss Chairperson? We take requests."

Like Courtenay a few minutes before, Delaney was speechless. This preschool rally would be better than she ever dreamed, with its beautiful banner, gaily colored balloons, and now the pep band to supply its own brand of magic. Delaney realized she wasn't the only one who was overcome. Both Courtenay and Pammi were staring at Mitch in sheer amazement.

"I can't believe it," Courtenay murmured. "Mitch Rhyner giving up his rock star image to help with the prom. It's like seeing a different person beneath the black leather jacket and heavy metal T-shirts."

"Whoever he is, I like it," Pammi said. "I like it a lot. And you do, too."

"Don't be ridiculous," Courtenay retorted. But Delaney saw her staring at Mitch with a softness in her eyes that hadn't been there before. And Pammi was looking at Tim a little differently since he decided to use her prom feature story in the *Bulletin*. There was something going on, all right, Delaney thought with a glow in her heart. Something to do with fantasy and enchantment. People were opening up more, becoming more vulnerable. Pammi had it right: Love *is* in the air.

Mitch's voice jerked her away from such romantic thoughts.

". . . or do we just stand around all day?"

She blinked at him. "I'm sorry, Mitch, what?"

"I said, do we strike up the band or do we just stand around all day?"

"He's waiting for you to give him some song titles," Courtenay offered.

"I'm glad someone's paying attention." Mitch smiled at Courtenay, and for the first time, a glimmer of a smile was mirrored on her face.

"Oh, we're all paying attention," Pammi said in a mock lecherous whisper. "Who wouldn't pay attention to such a hunk?" She nudged Courtenay, but Courtenay failed to respond. She was still staring at Mitch as if seeing him for the very first time.

Delaney scrambled in her head for songs. "Let's see, do you know any love themes from musicals or the movies? Oh, why am I drawing a blank? This is horrible!"

"Fight songs are more their style," Suzi said. "No offense, but I really doubt if the pep band can win over hearts with any mood music."

Delaney peered down the street. "We have to come up with something fast! Kids are starting to arrive!"

She stared in frustration at Mitch while the members of the band exchanged helpless glances. No one seemed to know any songs.

Out from behind the banner flew the large bumblebee. It quivered in midair for a second, then soared straight for Mitch, where it buzzed by his ear. Mitch put up his hands to wave the bee away, but suddenly clapped them in excitement instead.

"I've got it!" he exclaimed. "The perfect song! And the band knows it because they did it for the talent show in March. The Supremes classic from the sixties, 'Stop in the Name of Love.' "

" 'Stop in the Name of Love,' " Delaney repeated slowly. Her face brightened as if the sun had just come out. " 'Stop in the Name of Love' is absolutely perfect! Because that's what we want Claire and her Spirit Club to do before they ruin the prom. And it's what we're asking the juniors and seniors to do this morning, to stop and learn about the prom. Oh, Mitch, how did you ever come up with such a perfect choice?"

Mitch scratched his head, looking almost embarrassed. "You're not going to believe it, but that big bee going around my head a few seconds ago almost seemed to be humming, and what he seemed to be humming was . . .

well, cart me away to the nearest loony bin, but it sounded like the old Supremes hit."

"A Motown bee, that's rich." Pammi giggled.

Everyone laughed, Delaney the hardest. Honestly, the whole silly incident sounded exactly like one of her own butterfly tricks in the cupid-trainee days. This morning was turning out to be more crazy—and wonderful—than she had ever imagined. Mitch readied the band and counted off, "One, two, three . . ."

The pep band burst into "Stop in the Name of Love" as if they had been practicing for months. The sound was amazing. The volunteers stared at each other in delight while Mitch himself as honorary band director looked startled.

"This is going to work," Pammi said, tapping her feet to the music. "This is actually going to work."

"It can't get any better," Delaney agreed.

The first groups of students coming up to the entrance seemed bemused but all too willing to receive a flyer and ballot and hear about the upcoming vote for prom theme. Some of the kids shook their heads and just swept by, choosing to ignore the issue, but others stopped to hear the pep band and listen to Delaney and her friends. There was laughter, energy, and a sense of cooperative spiritedness about the rally. Several teachers came by to listen to the volunteers' spiel and to admire the banner and balloons. At one point the principal himself made a brief appearance and shook Delaney's hand.

"Too bad Claire isn't here to witness this," Pammi said with a laugh.

Delaney laughed with her. She thought she would burst with happiness. This was only day one of the Dream Scheme, and already there seemed to be genuine interest in her theme. Apathetic and bored about the prom?

Maybe the kids at Woodside had been like that last year, but last year a representative from the Love Bureau had not been organizing the event. This year's dance would shoot off more romantic sparks than a Fourth of July fireworks display.

She was right in the middle of handing out flyers, humming under her breath, when Pammi nudged her. "Look out; here comes trouble."

"Not trouble, just the competition," Delaney corrected firmly, as Claire swept through the crowd to the front door. "Now, be nice."

Claire was dressed as usual in men's clothes, a baggy pinstripe suit this time, and was surrounded by her friends, Dawn, Wendy, and Beth, as well as a number of drooling male admirers. She was recounting a joke, punctuating it with theatrical gestures, obviously trying to ignore the rally, but her friends pointed to the banner and balloons. Claire realized she had lost their attention and looked over at Delaney.

"Well, what do we have here?" she cooed, dripping venom. "How positively *enterprising* of you to make such a production out of such a simple issue. I *love* the poster, so sweet and childlike, like a Grandma Moses painting, and those balloons . . . just like the ones at my cousin's recent third birthday party."

Behind her Dawn, Wendy, and Beth were barely muffling sarcastic giggles.

"Of course," Claire swept right on, "if you have to advertise something so desperately, resorting to childish signs and music, then I'd say you were in trouble. The Spirit Club and the rest of the senior class know we're going to win with our theme, so why bother? It's really beneath us. But good luck, Delaney, you and all your little helpers. Even if your antics are such a waste of time."

Claire smiled sweetly. Pammi hissed, almost arching her back like a fighting cat, but Delaney looked Claire straight in the eye.

"We'll see what a waste of time these *antics* are when the junior and senior classes vote on Friday morning."

For a few tension-filled moments a subtle tug-of-war took place between the two girls as they locked glances. Then Claire looked away first, with an irritated toss of her head. She reached out and plucked a balloon from the ivy.

"This is what I think about your Dream Prom," she announced, green eyes narrowed. With a flick of her fingers, she released the helium balloon so that it sailed high into the sky. "Just a lot of hot air, I'm afraid."

And with a condescending smile, she sailed through the front door.

# The Spirit Club Strikes Back

*Up in the viewing room of the Love Bureau, Andrew was delivering a progress report to Valentina. As he talked, the Sweetheart Squadron Leader sat behind the ornate monitoring system and watched the tapes of Cupid Delaney's activities over the last two days. A crowd of cherubs and Senior Sweetheart members gathered around the screen, intrigued by the infamous cupid trainee's mission at Woodside High. No one had ever attempted to inject love and romance into such a large group before, and especially not teenagers, unpredictable and full of moods as they were. That was difficult enough. But to do it without using any celestial powers . . .? "Impossible," was the murmured consensus of most of those viewing the tapes.*

*"But you see it isn't!" Andrew argued with some heat. He pressed the pause button on the remote control and pointed to the still shot of an animated Cupid Delaney at Tuesday's before-school rally. "Look at the faces of those kids who are listening to Cupid Delaney. She's really got them motivated about the prom."*

*"And look at that cute bumblebee getting a free ride on the balloon right behind Cupid Delaney's head," one of the Senior Sweetheart members teased. "Seems as if he's pretty motivated, too."*

*Andrew wriggled a bit and quickly fast-forwarded the action.*

*"And here's the scene in the cafeteria yesterday. Cupid Delaney had volunteers putting chocolate kisses and candy hearts on every student's tray and—can we get the audio working?" Valentina adjusted a knob on the console. Instantly the viewing room was treated to a stereophonic rendition of Storm Devrie's hit, "Dream Only of Me," interspersed with the regular noise and clatter of a high school lunchroom. Andrew's face lit up with a proud grin.*

*"That was Cupid Delaney's doing as well. Bringing in the tape of their dance's theme song and persuading the cafeteria staff to break into the usual rock station to play it. Not once, I might add, but every ten minutes. By the end of the meal, three quarters of those kids walked out either humming or singing that song."*

*"And probably hating it, too, after all the repetition," Valentina murmured, lips twitching.*

*"Joke all you want," Andrew protested. "Cupid Delaney is really doing an extraordinary job. I've never seen a Love Bureau emissary throw herself so vigorously into an assignment before. She may not have magic at her disposal, but she's got ideas galore. For example, the hearts taped to every locker and the funny notices on the activities board that change every hour."*

*"The red and white color-coordinated outfits on the girls are a nice touch," Valentina admitted. "I see your clever cupid even managed to get some male school leaders to wear the Dream Team buttons. Now that takes a kind of magic all its own."*

*"You never know what to expect from Cupid Delaney," one of the younger cherubs piped up.*

*Squad Leader Amour closed her eyes and sighed. "An all-too-true comment." But in a second she was all business again. "Andrew, this is going so well for our little resident rebel—the growing momentum behind her campaign, the increasing awareness in the junior and senior classes. Is it going too well? I have to ask: Has Cupid Delaney ever cheated and used her powers?"*

*Andrew stiffened and stared down at the remote control in his*

70

*hand. Thoughts whirled crazily in his head. Now was no time to blurt out the truth about his "helping" Cupid Delaney. For Jupiter's sake, it wasn't like he entered the students' minds and transformed their thinking. He hadn't really altered anything major on this assignment, had he? Maybe an isolated hint to Mitch about a good song for the pep band, one or two bombing raids to direct Cupid Delaney to Helen's note cards about the prom or to startle the girl in the* Bulletin *office into losing Beth's prom article on the computer. But that was all. Nothing to enhance or falsify the kids' reactions to the Dream Prom campaign. That was all Cupid Delaney's doing, and he knew, absolutely, positively knew for a fact, that she had not gone back on her word and used her powers.*

*He returned a sharp-eyed Valentina's gaze without flinching. "I can honestly report that Cupid Delaney has used only mortal talents and capabilities, none borrowed from the Love Bureau. The success of the Dream Prom is hers, and hers alone."*

*The goddess played with the heart-shaped crystal locket around her neck and frowned. "Don't be so sure your cupid has succeeded in her mission. The junior and senior classes vote tomorrow morning. A lot can happen in eighteen hours. We might still hear from this notorious Claire Reggio and her Spirit Club."*

*"Cupid Delaney's assignments are always the most suspenseful," one of the cherubs exclaimed.*

*"It is strange that Claire hasn't done anything," Andrew said slowly. "She's watched Cupid Delaney organize all her meetings and arrange her stunts, and she always walks by whatever event Cupid Delaney has planned with a superior smile on her face. As if . . . as if"—the blond-haired boy groped for the right words, while Valentina put two and two together and finished the sentence for him—"as if she had a scheme of her own and knew Cupid Delaney couldn't possibly win."*

*Andrew stared at Valentina in disbelief. "But the only thing left in Cupid Delaney's campaign is the special cheerleading*

71

*presentation and fashion show she's putting on after school today. If Claire's going to move, it's got to be then."*

*Valentina peered out the window at the sundial in the administration building's courtyard. "Then? You mean now, I think. Doesn't Woodside's final bell ring at two-thirty? It's two-twenty-five, Andrew."*

*"Oh, no! I've got to get down there and find Claire and see if she's up to something."*

*"Well, if she is, just remember one thing. Cupid Delaney has to fight Claire Reggio, not you."*

*In a snap, the athletic boy transformed himself into a bumblebee and buzzed straight out the open window.*

*Valentina Amour gazed at all her Love Bureau colleagues, whose jaws had dropped and eyes widened at Andrew's dramatic exit.*

*"Mark my words, there's going to be trouble," the goddess observed with a gleam in her eye. "Now let's see how our rebellious cupid handles it."*

*"Oh, I told you Cupid Delaney's assignments are always the most exciting and action-packed!" cried the cherub.*

*Everyone eagerly clustered around the monitoring screen as Valentina adjusted the picture and a very distraught Delaney came into focus.*


She was pacing up and down by the makeshift runway Mitch and his Service Commission volunteers had erected just that afternoon next to the quad's fountain. The three-tiered stone fountain was known as the principal's baby because he had persuaded the parent-teacher association that Woodside's grounds needed beautification. But the fountain was flawed. It never operated properly. Consequently, a frustrated Mr. Karger ordered that it never be turned on, even in the mild spring months. The fountain became a nonfunctioning piece of statuary, but one that the principal forbade the students to touch. The fountain was still Mr. Karger's baby.

It did not sprinkle water, but it made a nice centerpiece for Delaney's fashion show, and she and a small group of her friends paced in front of it. They watched the grassy area fill up with laughing, excited kids. Delaney looked at her watch again and ran a hand nervously through her blonde curls.

"It's almost two-thirty, the show's about to start, and where is everybody?"

"You've got a good crowd," Courtenay tried to reassure her. "Granted, there are lots more juniors than seniors, but that's to be expected with Claire pulling the senior strings."

"She's not talking about the audience, you dummy," Pammi exclaimed. "She means the performers."

"You mean the models Tatters sent over aren't dressed yet?" Courtenay asked.

"Dressed yet? They're not even here!" Delaney moaned. "Mrs. Simon told me they never arrived. They were supposed to change inside Mrs. Simon's staff room."

"We've got to think of something!" Courtenay stared at each of her friends but gave Mitch the full beam of her big, imploring eyes.

The dark-haired boy gave a helpless shrug. "Hey, I'm no miracle worker. I can't say a few magic words and produce those models."

"Delaney persuaded the owner of Tatters to hire models for our Dream Prom fashion show," Courtenay explained. "It's at no cost to us because the models will be wearing gowns from the store. It's like an advertising gimmick, I guess. And it really would have been the best promotion for our theme, but now—"

"Well, don't talk as if it's the past tense, for heaven's

sake!" snapped Pammi. "We can salvage things, can't we, Delaney?"

Delaney thought furiously for a moment, failing to notice the large bumblebee that circled the length of the quad, as if searching for someone, and then headed for the parking lot. She suddenly straightened, her eyes filled with determination. All traces of earlier nervousness were gone.

"Pammi, you go get the junior varsity cheerleaders and tell them there's been a change in plan. They're to come out first, not after the fashion show. Okay?"

Pammi snapped to attention and grinned. "Very much okay!" She ran to the gym.

"Courtenay, could you take care of the sound system? John brought in a tape deck, and it's got all the songs for the cheerleaders. Huey Lewis's 'Power of Love' should kick off the rally on the right note."

Courtenay's frown lifted. "Should I start it now?"

"Why not? It's two-thirty. Let's get the show on the road."

While Courtenay hurried to find John and start the music, Delaney dug into her bag and fished out several small boxes containing toy thermometers. "Tim, could you do the honors of getting some volunteers to pass these thermometers out? And when they hand them to kids, be sure to tell them to say, 'Catch Dream Prom fever!' "

Tim took the boxes and examined the contents. "You sure are something, Delaney. Has anyone ever told you that before?"

Many times, Delaney wanted to say, remembering all the lectures and sermons she had received from the Love Bureau. But she only shook her head and laughed. Tim enlisted the aid of some *Bulletin* staff members and began to distribute the gag gifts.

"Hey, don't forget about me," Mitch said. "I want to help, too." He was on duty as a Service Commissioner and was wearing his official cap and commission jacket.

Delaney eyed the swelling, noisy crowd. Kids were still laughing and talking, making jokes about the toy thermometers, but they were getting impatient. The good mood wouldn't last forever. In another few minutes they'd start protesting or clapping. Delaney knew what Mitch could do.

"You take charge of the crowd," she instructed Mitch, "and see that they don't get out of hand, and I'll take charge of the show. Is that fair enough?"

"Sounds good to me, as long as you be sure to tell Courtenay what a good job I'm doing."

"I think she knows by now," Delaney said with a grin. Mitch smiled in return and began to round up fellow Service Commissioners who were sprawled on the grass or sitting on the quad ledge to watch the action.

Pammi stuck her head out of the gym and waved. The junior varsity cheerleaders were ready.

Courtenay and John gave the signal, too.

Delaney took a deep breath and tried to calm her racing heart. Please let this work, she silently prayed. Please don't let it fall apart at the last minute as so many of my other assignments have. Let this be the one that wins me my Dream Prom *and* my wings.

She waved first to Pammi and then to Courtenay. With a pounding beat, a roll of drums, the music started. The crowd roared in approval, and the junior varsity cheerleaders came bounding out of the gym into the cleared area before the fountain and went right into the routines Delaney had helped them choreograph, high kicking and turning cartwheels.

"Perfect! It's terrific!" Delaney cried enthusiastically as

Pammi, John, and Courtenay raced over to join her. "Everyone loves it!"

A madly waving Helen pushed her way through the crowd to get to Delancy. "Delaney, the models just arrived! They're in Mrs. Simon's office right now, changing!"

Delaney let out a joyous whoop and jumped in the air.

"We're going to do it!" she cried, hugging each of her friends in turn. "This one's going to go off without a single hitch!"

*Unfortunately, Andrew was hearing a distinctly different verdict from the Spirit Club. After circling the entire school, he had finally located his elusive quarry. Claire and Dawn were perched on Claire's car in the school parking lot, acting like they didn't have a care in the world. They were leaning back against the windshield, sunglasses on, trying to catch some sun. Andrew landed on top of the fiery red Trans Am and edged as close to the two girls as he safely could without them hearing his buzzing. Fortunately, the car stereo was blasting, and Claire and Dawn were singing along to the top 40 songs when Storm Devrie's "Dream Only of Me" came on.*

*Instantly Claire stiffened and sat up.*

*"Should I turn that disgusting song off?" Dawn asked. "Lord knows we've had it up to our eyeballs this week."*

*But Claire experienced an abrupt change of heart. She pulled her sunglasses off and twirled them almost gaily in her hand. "Why bother? After our bombshell this afternoon, we'll never have to hear that odious number again. So let's enjoy it for the last time, knowing it's not Delaney's theme song but her swan song."*

*Dawn laughed but then nibbled at a fingernail. "Are you sure we won't get into trouble with our plan, Claire? I mean, I want to graduate and go to college, I really do."*

"Relax. Nobody's going to get into trouble—except our little Love Bug Gang. Because in another five minutes, maybe less, their prom campaign's history. And the senior class, led by the Spirit Club, will take over the prom, the way I intended it. This is my dance, Dawn, no one else's. I created the concept, I got the bands, I talked to the country club. No minor-league social zero like Delaney is going to take my evening away from me."

"I can hardly wait," Dawn said. "I want to be there when Delaney and her friends see what we've cooked up."

"Very soon now," Claire assured her, checking her watch. "The word will come any minute."

Andrew buzzed back and forth on the red roof of the car, upset and nervous. What word was Claire talking about? What would happen very soon? And why would Cupid Delaney's campaign be history?

Seconds later a yellow Camaro roared into the parking lot and squealed to a stop next to the Trans Am. Wendy and Beth jumped out, their faces flushed and their eyes shining with excitement.

"Operation Mile High just got off the ground," Beth announced. "Everything went off on schedule. And can you believe it? My aunt actually thanked me for the chance to get her club up in the air and performing again. She says once kids see what she can do, she'll be working at all kinds of functions—birthdays, graduation parties, you name it."

Claire nudged Dawn in high good humor and slid off the car. "We really lucked out. We got for free what would have cost us a year's allowance! And I can't wait to see Delaney's reaction to our high-flying surprise. Very soon it'll be farewell, Shirley Temple, once and for all, and farewell, Dream Prom."

"And hello, Mogul Madness and Puttin' on the Glitz," chimed in Wendy.

Together the four girls hurried over to the quad, giggling and whispering.

*Andrew didn't hesitate. He took off and soared after them, hoping it would not be too late.*

The fashion show had just started, to cheers, wolf whistles, and wild applause. Delaney had almost persuaded herself to relax and stop worrying when the first sign of disaster struck.

"Up there!" one of the kids in the audience shouted and pointed. "In the sky!"

Heads turned away from the runway, focused upward. A small plane was circling overhead, a long banner flapping behind it. The plane dipped its wings as if to acknowledge the kids' growing attention and swooped lower.

"Hey, what's the banner say?"

"Can you make it out?"

Craig Lacrosse stood up, a cocky grin on his face. "It says: *Power is the ultimate high.*"

"Huh?"

One by one the kids repeated the words, trying to figure it out, much to Delaney's dismay. Although many didn't know what it meant, she did. Claire had gotten this plane to buzz the quad and draw attention away from her fashion show. Claire had waited until the last minute and timed it perfectly. The two models halted on their way down the runway, looking uncertainly over at Delaney. No one paid them the least bit of attention, not when a low-flying aircraft was practically waggling its tail and playing tricks for the students.

Pammi and Courtenay rushed to Delaney's side. "What's going on?"

"It's show time, Claire Reggio style."

"But she's not even here."

Delaney made a face. "Count on it, she's here. And so

*78*

are her cronies. They wouldn't miss a chance to witness one-upmanship with me."

Pammi craned her head around, surveyed the crowd. "But I don't see—oh, you're right. They *are* here. Claire and her Spirit Club snakettes are lurking by the back ledge with malicious smiles on their overly made-up faces."

"I don't think Mr. Karger's going to appreciate the aerial stunt," Courtenay observed sourly.

"It doesn't matter what the principal thinks; it's what the kids think," Delaney said, "and the kids are getting a kick out of it."

Without warning, a figure dropped out of the plane, followed by another and another. At each new skydiver's appearance, the kids jumped up and roared. By now all attention to the Dream Prom fashion show had evaporated. The models strode off the runway, looking irked, and returned to the school to change.

"I can't blame them." Delaney sighed. "What a fiasco."

The skydivers linked arms in a circle and swirled almost magically against the sky before they opened their parachutes. Claire walked purposefully to the front of the fountain, where Delaney stood with her friends.

"Nice fashion show," Claire remarked with a false smile. "But it's a shame it didn't last long."

Someone had cut the music, and Claire put her fingers in her mouth and whistled. It was piercing and sharp and would have stopped a taxi in a blizzard in New York. Amazingly, everyone stopped talking and swiveled around to face Claire. Used to being in the limelight, she grinned unself-consciously and held up her hands.

"I'm Claire Reggio and I'm president of the Spirit Club, for all of you who don't know me."

"Who doesn't know the drama queen!" one of the senior boys called, and everyone laughed.

"Well, I'm also trying to organize the junior/senior prom this year, and contrary to what you've been hearing all this week and especially today, I say we forget all the cutesy greeting-card sentiments of a Dream Prom and . . . *get down to business!*"

From out of the gym poured senior varsity cheerleaders, dressed identically in navy business suits and running shoes and carrying briefcases. Two by two they power-walked in a circle around the laughing, whistling crowd. Then they headed for the front, where they executed a "Mega-mega-mega Mogul Madness" cheer, hurling their briefcases in the air for a finale. The cases burst open, spilling green pieces of paper all over that looked amazingly like . . .

"Money!" one of the boys in the crowd yelled. "It's money!"

Bills of all denominations lay scattered on the ground like confetti. Before anyone could move, a large bumblebee zoomed straight over the area and instantly, incredibly, a strong wind picked up most of the bills and swept them along to the very edge of the fountain. The crowd stared at the tantalizing sight of the green tornado with hungry eyes and open mouths.

"C'mon, let's get it!"

Claire and Delaney found themselves backed against the very edge of the fountain with the weight of the money-hungry mob pressing against them.

"Wait!" Claire shrieked. "It isn't real! It's play money! It's play money!"

No one heard her over the commotion. Delaney tried to keep her balance as arms and bodies thrust past her to catch the bills. And then an amazing thing happened.

The bumblebee circled past the fountain, and as it soared overhead, water began spurting out of the dry stone. At first in trickles, and then gathering force, jets of water cascaded crazily over the crowd.

Delaney caught Claire's eye and smiled sweetly at the furious, trapped, very soaked girl.

"How positively *enterprising* of you to make such a production out of such a simple issue," she said, repeating Claire's earlier jibes about the Dream Prom rally. "I thought such *childish* antics were beneath the Spirit Club."

"Why, you little . . ." Claire sputtered, face flushed in embarrassed fury. Claire reached over to push Delaney into the water, but a tall, blond-haired boy appeared out of nowhere and caught Delaney around the waist. Losing her balance, Claire teetered on the edge of the fountain and crashed into the water with a banshee screech. Student after squealing student followed suit until the entire fountain was filled with thrashing bodies.

Delaney turned and got a good look at her rescuer. It was the same boy she had met Monday in the hallway.

"You!" she exclaimed. She was breathing quickly, aware of a wonderful lightness of spirit. "Who are you?"

He reflected a moment, smiling warmly into her eyes. "Who am I? Just someone who likes to wing it, I guess."

She turned away for a second, peering down at a very soaked Claire, who was still wailing in childish rage.

"Our ideas may have been so much hot air to you and your high and mighty Spirit Club," Delaney said, wagging a playful finger at her arch nemesis, "but yours, my dear Ms. Reggio, are definitely *all wet.*"

# Cupid Delaney Rallies

By Saturday afternoon the events of the last two days seemed even grimmer to Delaney. She walked along the main street in town, heading for Pammi's house and the Dream Club meeting. With feet dragging, eyes downcast, she was too wrapped up in gloomy thoughts to think about Storm Devrie or to window-shop, a favorite pastime. How could it have happened? she asked herself yet one more time. How could she have failed her mission so abysmally? Perhaps technically she had not really failed because the kids never got the chance to vote, but there was to be no Dream Prom at Woodside High this year.

No Dream Prom, or Power Prom either, for that matter.

Mr. Karger had witnessed the scene in the fountain Thursday afternoon from his top-floor window, and that had made up his mind. On Friday morning he had called a special assembly for the junior and senior classes and told them in no uncertain terms what he thought of their crazy, undisciplined behavior. The battle between the proms had gotten out of hand, he said. There would be no dance on May 26 as originally planned. He was sorry, but he just couldn't see any other way to get his message across. End of conversation. Assembly dismissed.

Claire and Delaney sat on opposite sides of the auditorium in stunned silence. Delaney's friends had rallied around her. Claire's Spirit Club had rallied around her, but it was no good. Love and romance had fallen by the wayside, and consequently Delaney would lose any final chance to earn her wings.

And equally as devastating, Delancy realized, slouching along Main Street, she and Alvin would never get to go to their junior/senior prom. On her very last day as a mortal being, she would not have the thrill or the pleasure of attending the most romantic event of a teenage girl's life. She and Alvin would not have their last special evening after all.

In rotten spirits, she approached Tatters. The same two mannequins were in the front window.

"Oh, Valentina, I'm so sorry," Delaney whispered, staring into the unanimated face of the female mannequin. "I know you can't hear me, but I really did it this time; I botched up my last mission and ruined the prom for the whole school. If I hadn't tried to outdo myself on all the events and rallies, Claire wouldn't have had to come back and show me what she could do—oh, it's a mess and I'm sorry, I'm really sorry. Now I'll never earn my wings and be a cupid."

*"Look at that poor thing." Bella Rosa sighed, raising an eyebrow. "She's really in trouble."*

*The two other Senior Sweetheart leaders in the viewing room peered over at the monitor. "Are you watching Cupid Delaney?"*

*"It's so sad. She's practically in tears because the Woodside prom was canceled by the principal."*

*"Oh, no." The three Love Bureau demigoddesses looked at one*

*another in alarm. "If she fails this mission, it's her last. And you know what happens to cupid trainees who fail their assignments. They're either reduced to lowly cherub status, peeling grapes and chocolate kisses, and cleaning wings, or else they're kicked out of the bureau. And once they land as mortals on earth, it's terribly hard to find jobs that suit their limited talents. What's open for these poor outcasts except writing cutesy, romantic greeting-card lines or tutoring poetry appreciation to indifferent or hostile students? Oh, it's too unpleasant to think about. I just hope Valentina doesn't find out."*

*"Find out what?" the Love Bureau administrator queried in a sharp voice as she burst into the viewing room. "What am I not supposed to know?"*

*"It's Cupid Delaney," Passionata murmured. "The poor thing is in a state because the prom was called off. She's really upset, Valentina. Look at her yourself. She's lost all hope. She's given up."*

*"Given up? GIVEN UP?" Valentina's voice rose. She stared at the screen and at the disconsolate figure of Cupid Delaney. "That doesn't sound like our little rebel at all. Why, she can't give up. Not if she wants to fly up in June. Doesn't the ninny know she has to fight? The battle may be lost, but the war isn't over yet!"*

*"Tell her that," urged the three demigoddesses. "Give her a sign."*

*Valentina thought for a few moments, then sorrowfully shook her head. "It's not something I should have to tell her. It's something she has to learn herself. She has to bounce back, our dejected Cupid Delaney. But if she doesn't, well . . ." She raised her hands in a meaningful gesture, then slowly let them fall.*

*All four watched the screen with rapt attention as . . .*


. . . tears formed in Delaney's eyes. Her lower lip quivered uncontrollably. Through her blurred vision she almost thought she saw the lips of the blond-haired male mannequin quirk in a sympathetic smile. But that was absurd, of course. She was really letting her imagination play tricks on her. Still . . . there was something about the mannequin's features that rang a bell in her head. Something about them that looked very familiar, but try as she might, she couldn't figure it out.

I'm going crazy, she thought, smiling through her tears. I'm having a Love Bureau breakdown. Embarrassed to be making a display of herself, she hurriedly wiped her eyes and blew her nose. Just in time, too, as someone behind her called her name. Turning, she spotted Alvin in his VW. He double-parked in front of Tatters and leaned across the seat.

"Need a ride over to Pammi's?"

Normally the sight of Alvin made her smile, but this afternoon his cheerful, carefree face didn't work its usual magic on her. She felt too depressed.

"Thanks, but I want to walk. I'm hoping the fresh air will pick up my spirits."

Alvin gave her a sympathetic smile. "I thought you'd be feeling down after Karger's announcement yesterday, so I . . . ah . . ."—he hesitated, blushed—"bought you a little something to cheer you up."

She felt a warm glow burn through the clouds. "Oh, Alvin, you shouldn't have!"

He fumbled in his pocket and handed her a small box. The bow was crookedly tied, but Delaney didn't care. Trust Alvin to think of her feelings at a time like this.

"Go on, open it," Alvin urged. "It's a cheer-up present, but it's also a six-month anniversary gift. I hope you like it."

"Oh, Alvin . . ." Eyes sparkling, she undid the bow and

opened the box. Nestled inside tissue paper was a delicate gold charm bracelet. She held it up with a delighted cry.

"See, I chose six charms to symbolize each of our months together," Alvin explained. "The miniature train was for our November date to the Model Engineers' Exhibit, and the skates were for our adventure at the rink in December. The Statue of Liberty was from our trip to New York in January . . ."

Delaney jingled each of the charms as he pointed them out, smiling with pleasure. Trust Alvin to celebrate their anniversary in such a special way.

"I'll pick six more charms to complete the bracelet for our first year together," Alvin said.

But there would be no more charms on her bracelet. Delaney would not see Alvin again after May. Her good mood was shattered. If only there could be a happy ending for everyone, for Alvin as well as herself.

Before she could say anything, Alvin suddenly turned his head and beeped his horn. "Look, there's Helen, crossing the street."

"She's on her way to Pammi's, I bet," Delaney said. She called to the girl, who glanced over at them with a start and a funny look on her face.

But she was not going to Pammi's, it turned out. She had an English assignment she hadn't finished, she nervously explained to Delaney, and had to forego the pleasure of watching five solid hours of Storm Devrie in "The Young Dreamers" in order to study at the library.

"But you told me you finished the paper on Joseph Conrad," Delaney questioned her.

Helen was stammering out a lame explanation when a silver Fiat tried to pass Alvin's double-parked car and failed. The driver beeped angrily and stuck his head out the window.

"It's Craig!" Helen squeaked. She practically dropped the books in her arms.

"Oh, for pity's sake, don't faint at the sight of the great senior god,"Alvin growled.

"You'd better move your car; he can't get by," Helen said, totally oblivious to Alvin's sarcastic remark. A dazed look had come into her eyes as she stared over at the Fiat.

"Go ahead, Alvin," Delaney seconded.

But Alvin's face took on a stubborn cast she knew all too well.

"I'm not budging. Let him go around."

"Alvin!" Helen pleaded, but to no avail. Alvin would not give way.

The silver Fiat laboriously edged alongside the VW. Craig angrily leaned across the front seat to blast Alvin when he caught sight of Helen. Immediately hostility turned into playboy charm.

"Hey, how's my favorite girl?"

"Uh, fine." Helen melted beneath his gaze.

"Listen, sweet one, I'm going to need that paper on Conrad by Monday morning, so be sure I get it before first period, all right?"

Helen stared into Craig's blue eyes and shook her head up and down like a puppet. The senior awarded her a wink and a grin before roaring off.

"Sweet one?" Alvin repeated in an outraged voice. "He called you sweet one? And favorite girl? And then has the colossal nerve to dump his assignment on you?"

Helen shuffled on the sidewalk, her cheeks turning pink. "You don't understand."

"No, I don't!" Alvin yelled. "I don't understand." He pounded on the steering wheel in baffled fury. "How can you even like a lump of brainless protoplasm like Craig Lacrosse, let alone do his homework for him? You dated him once. You of all people should know what a jerk he is."

Helen's square little chin lifted defiantly. "You just stop it, Alvin. Just mind your own business. You've never understood how I've felt about Craig and that's too bad but I'm doing what I want. Do you hear me? What I want."

Delaney reached out to touch the girl's trembling shoulders. "Listen, Helen. Alvin didn't mean anything—"

"The heck I didn't!" Alvin shouted. "I meant every word!"

"He's mad because he knows you really don't want to be doing Craig's homework on a weekend night. And I know it too. Wouldn't you rather be at the Dream Club meeting? Courtenay said she got the autographed pictures from the soap today. She said the ones of Storm are unbelievable."

"Really? The pictures arrived?" Helen's face lit up momentarily, then darkened again. "I—I'm sorry, Delaney, but I can't go tonight. I have to do this paper for Craig. I have to. If I don't . . ."

"If you don't, what?" Delaney asked softly. "He'll never speak to you again? He'll cut you dead at Spirit Club meetings?"

"Whoopee, a big loss," Alvin interjected. "You'd really be missing out."

"Alvin!" Delaney turned on him, but it was too late. Helen had squeezed her eyes shut, shaking her head from side to side. She refused to listen anymore.

Delaney tried to reach her one more time. "Please, Helen, we'll really miss you if you don't make the meeting. And Craig should know better than to take advantage of you. It really isn't fair."

Helen's eyes flew open. "Fair? I know it isn't fair, but

it's something I have to do. You two don't understand. You're lucky. You have each other, the perfect couple. But I don't have anyone, no one. And having Craig this way is better than not having anybody at all . . . Oh, what's the use!"

With a strangled cry, Helen pushed past Delaney and hurried off.

"Some help you were," Delaney rebuked Alvin, but he didn't hear her. He was staring after Helen's departing figure with a worried look on his face.

"I should go after her and apologize," he said. "I'm sorry, Delaney, I think I better—"

He started the car and, with a distracted wave to Delaney, pulled into traffic.

Delaney stood on the sidewalk, head reeling. Had she imagined it, or had calm, even-tempered, unflappable Alvin Danziger flown off the handle just now and yelled at Helen? And had quiet, fade-into-the-woodwork Helen Mapes actually gotten angry enough to tell Alvin to mind his own business? She was still trying to figure it out when a trio of girls from Woodside High came swinging down the street and stopped in front of Tatters' window.

"Look at that drop-dead black number on the rack over there," one of them said in a wistful voice. "That would be such a dynamite dress for the prom."

"Well, forget it," one of the girls said. "There isn't going to be a prom, remember?"

"But it could have been so much fun, especially since I just started seeing Barry."

"Yeah, and Tom and I got back together."

"We could have triple-dated."

The girls looked at one another glumly and walked past the store.

A shaken Delaney remained behind, the unhappy faces

of the girls still lingering in her mind. There were students at Woodside High who wanted the prom, and now they would be cheated out of a chance to experience one. What can I do? Delaney thought in frustration. I blew any chances of giving them a Dream Prom. It's too late to do anything. Too late . . .

*"It's not too late," Passionata said in the viewing room, eyes glued to the girl's face. "It's not."*

*"Come on, Cupid Delaney. Show us what you're made of. Prove you're worthy of being in the Love Bureau." Enchantée secretly crossed her fingers behind her back, not wanting Valentina to make fun of her. But the Love Bureau administrator was too intent upon the screen to notice her colleague's superstitious habit.*

*"It's now or never," the goddess intoned. "She falls or flies on what she does next." Valentina leaned forward and held her breath.*

*The three Senior Sweetheart members held their breath.*

A bumblebee crawling to the top of a parking meter right behind Delaney held its breath.

Delaney swung around to face the Tatters' window display and addressed the Valentina look-alike mannequin.

"I've been facing the wrong way," she said in a breathless voice. "Looking at my problems from the wrong end of the telescope. Instead of whining, 'What can I do about the prom?,' what I should be saying is 'How can I *not* do anything?' Am I crazy or what?" She tapped her forehead and burst into an infectious laugh that made the plump bumblebee break into a little impromptu dance on the top of the parking meter.

"I mean, do I have a reputation to uphold inside the Northeast Division of the Love Bureau or not? Am I not well known as a freethinker, a maverick, a rebel? Can I

even begin to imagine a life without certified cupid wings and romantic purpose? Before I bite the Love Bureau bullet, before I give up on my skills and my *chutzpah* and my imagination, I'm going to give it one more shot. I'm going to fight and I'm going to plan and I'm going to protest. And before I'm done, Woodside High will have its Dream Prom or they'll have to bury me beside that fountain!"

Delaney concluded her little pep talk with a leap and a twirl, a bumblebee buzzing by providing the applause . . .

. . . *while three demigoddesses and one full-blooded goddess high above sighed in collective relief and burst into smiles. Cupid Delaney was back. Watch out, Woodside High.*

# The Revolting Juniors

Delaney had planned carefully.

She had spent Saturday night and all day Sunday talking to her friends, working out her idea. Now, Monday morning at 10:30, she was ready. The stage was set. She and the faithful few who agreed to join her were hovering just inside the gym doors, ready to march onto the football field, where the school photographer was trying to assemble the senior class for the official yearbook picture. The fourth-year students scrambled around the bleachers, refusing to sit still in the balmy sunshine, while behind them waited the pep band and a number of other school organizations and clubs. The field was a madhouse. Supervising teachers blew whistles and ran back and forth with clipboards, futilely trying to maintain order for the photographic sessions.

Inside the shelter of the gym, Pammi examined her friends with raised eyebrows. "I don't know what the rest of you guys think, but I'd say we're revolting."

"Revolting is not quite the word I'd use," Delaney corrected with a grin. "I'd call it protesting."

"Protesting, revolting, whatever, we're still planning to march out there before half of the entire school and tell

the world what we think. I'm sure Claire and her fanatical Spirit Club followers will have something to say about that." Pammi paused, eyes glinting. "And I say, let's go get 'em!"

"Yeah," another voice chimed in, "it's now or never. Before we lose our nerve."

With a wildly beating heart and a silent prayer, Delaney led the way onto the playing field. Pammi, Courtenay, and five other volunteers followed. As they neared the bleachers, they each held up their signs as prearranged. The photographer fiddled with his camera in front of the students, oblivious to the eight new arrivals, but the seniors immediately stopped primping in mirrors and combing their hair to point at the unusual sight.

"Hey, get a load of that!"

"What are they doing?"

"They're picketing, for cripe's sake!"

"What are they picketing for?"

The girls stopped, silently holding up each sign so it could be read.

"We're RAD, Romantics Against Discrimination."

"We're JADED, Juniors Against the Denial of Elegant Dances."

"Have a Heart; Save Our Prom."

The kids read the signs aloud, broke out into laughter, argument, and heated discussion.

"Go for it, Delaney!" yelled Mitch, jumping to his feet near the top of the bleachers and clapping. "I'm with you!"

"Yeah, so am I," Tim concurred. He stood up amidst assorted boos, yells, and cheers. "Don't you guys want a prom?"

"Aw, sit down, Bratt," someone jeered. "You're always standing up for some darn issue."

But Suzi Ramos got to her feet, nudged her friends, and they followed suit, as did most of the seniors on the *Bulletin* staff. Then Mitch's fellow Service Commissioners stood up, too.

The photographer, a tubby little man with a nervous facial tic, threw up his hands. "All right, people, *what* is going on here? You're bobbing up and down like jack-in-the-boxes. Everyone sit! Sit, sit, sit!"

One of the teachers hurried over. "What's the problem? What's happening?"

Claire jumped to her feet and pointed at Delaney. "The problem is Delaney Smith and her deranged group of juniors. They think their little stunt is clever, but it's ruining our class picture. This is the seniors' time and the seniors' picture and she shouldn't be here creating a scene."

Delaney paused in her walking to confront Claire. "I hardly think quietly holding a sign that displays my beliefs is creating a scene. Jumping up and screaming at the top of your lungs and pointing your finger at me is, however."

Several of the kids laughed. Claire's green eyes narrowed.

"Listen, you jabbering junior, you just clear off. Do you understand me? This is senior property and senior time."

Delaney beamed angelically and continued to pace with her friends. Meanwhile, a plump bumblebee sunning in the grass near the bleachers took off in the direction of the administration building. Seconds later he had wriggled through the open window of the principal's office and buzzed around Mr. Karger's slightly balding head. The principal had been lecturing Trip Hawkins for yet another infraction of the rules when the bee zigzagged through the air and caught his eye. Instantly the lecture died on Mr. Karger's lips. He stuttered to a complete stop like a run-down battery-operated toy. Frowning in a puzzled way, he swiveled around in his chair to stare out the window at the playing field. Seconds stretched into minutes and still he stared. Behind him Trip Hawkins coughed, banged his boots on the floor, muttered under his breath. The principal of Woodside High paid no attention to him.

"Mrs. Tapley," Mr. Karger finally called, "come in here, please."

When the principal's secretary hurried in, the bumble-bee soared out the window and flew straight back to the playing field.

*Andrew landed on the photographer's camera case, humming in high spirits and anticipation. Shouldn't be long now, he thought, mentally rubbing his hands together. What Cupid Delaney started, I can help finish. He crawled back and forth on the black leather case, too keyed up to just sit back and enjoy the show.*

*And no doubt about it, Cupid Delaney had done it again. Had stirred up dialogue and dissension among the two upper classes. But at least it centered on the prom. She hadn't thrown in the towel, and she was making the students see that they didn't have to, either. They had a voice in the matter. If they wanted to enjoy a prom this Saturday night, they had to get their heads out of the sand and ask for one. From where Andrew sat, it looked like a good portion of the junior class was backing Delaney. I wish Valentina could see this! Andrew thought proudly. Talk about the right spirit. And it was all Cupid Delaney's doing.*

To the supervising teachers' consternation and surprise, many of the third-year students had broken ranks with the clubs and organizations waiting in line to be photo-

95

graphed and joined Delaney in her protest. Pammi had come up with the idea of having the kids form a moving heart and, laughing now, getting into the spirit, many of the students moved into the correct formation and began marching and chanting, "Have a heart, save our prom!"

"It's not your prom, you know," one of the seniors cried from the bleachers. "You don't own it."

"Then come down and join us," Pammi invited. "Let's make this the biggest moving heart on record!"

"If this isn't the most pathetic protest I've ever seen," Claire announced in a disgusted voice. "They think they're RAD? They're not RAD; they're sad. Now can we get back to having our yearbook picture taken?"

Discussions, some heated, some humorous, broke out in the bleachers. Much to Claire's obvious irritation, a group of laughing seniors scrambled onto the field and joined ranks with the juniors. The ever-moving heart began to swell.

The photographer slumped on the bench, morosely cradling his head in his hands. He had given up. The teachers vainly blew whistles, tried to order the kids back to their places, but eventually they, too, eyed the prom protest with resigned smiles and good-natured shrugs that only annoyed Claire more.

"Can't you teachers stop this ridiculous parade so we can have our picture taken?" Claire demanded.

"What do you suggest we do?" one of the teachers asked.

Claire sputtered and fumed. She and Dawn, Wendy, and Beth bent their heads together like the witches plotting evil in *Macbeth*.

A visibly nervous Helen edged out of the Chess Club to join the heart. Claire tried to impale her with an icy stare, but Helen kept her head down and continued walking.

"Helen, over here!" Delaney shouted, indicating an opening in the heart next to Pammi and Courtenay.

Claire turned to her friends. "I can't believe my eyes! Helen Mapes coming out of the closet to make a statement. This is really going to cost her her reelection to the Spirit Club next year."

Helen overheard the remark and hesitated. Just then Alvin hurried over to join her. Giving him a nervous but grateful smile, Helen led the way onto the field, where the two of them joined the heart next to Pammi and Courtenay.

Claire sat down abruptly, muttering under her breath, only to rise seconds later, a triumphant gleam in her eyes, when someone cried, "Mr. Karger's secretary is coming this way!"

The principal's secretary. That could only mean one thing. A summons to his office. A buzz spread through the bleachers.

The moving heart began to falter. The chanting wavered. Mrs. Tapley cut across the field, and as soon as she reached the bleachers, everything died. The kids became perfectly still.

Mrs. Tapley planted herself before the heart. "Who's responsible for this?" she asked in a no-nonsense tone of voice.

There was only a moment's hesitation before Delaney stepped out of the formation. "I am."

"So am I," announced Pammi and stepped forward.

"Me, too," said a pale Courtenay.

About thirty kids clustered protectively around Delaney, but it was only Delaney that Mrs. Tapley ordered to follow her.

"Mr. Karger is most anxious to talk to you," the secretary said.

Delaney swallowed, but, chin lifted, readily followed the woman off the field.

Her friends stared forlornly after her.

"Good luck, Delaney!" Pammi called.

"Luck?" Claire's lips curved in a satisfied smile. "She's going to need more than that when Karger's finished with her."

*Andrew buzzed in an agitated fashion on the camera case. Had he done the right thing in alerting the principal? Had he assessed the situation properly? What if the whole thing blew up in Cupid Delaney's face?*

*He quickly took off and soared straight for the administration building.*

*"Good luck, Cupid Delaney," Andrew whispered under his breath.*

# Getting the Scoop

Delaney called an emergency meeting immediately after school. The individuals most active on her Dream Team assembled for sundaes and other gooey concoctions at Le Scoop, the best dessert place in the Woodside Mall. Delaney held court in the large back booth, a chocolate ice cream soda in front of her. Pammi, Courtenay, and Alvin had settled for other calorically rich items, like the freshly baked chocolate chip cookies and the vanilla frosted brownies.

"I still can't believe the good news," Courtenay said, brownie crumbs dotting her lip. "I mean, it's so incredible."

"I told you to think positive," Pammi retorted. "Haven't I always told you that, Wilcox?"

"I know, I know, it's just that I expected Mr. Karger to suspend Delaney after she saw him this morning and instead, wow . . ."

Delaney put down her spoon and laughed. "*Wow* is the right word. I'm still in shock. Can you believe it? We're actually allowed to hold a dance this Saturday night. Granted, it can't be a prom. He still won't allow that, but at least he's letting us organize a dance. And all because

Mr. Karger said he liked my spirit and the way both the junior and senior classes were cooperating in making the huge heart on the football field."

"Cooperating?" Alvin snorted. "It's obvious he wasn't there to hear the drama queen. Talk about making a fool of herself."

Pammi nodded. "Not to mention having the nerve to threaten Helen right in front of everyone. That was really nice of you, Alvin, to come forward when you did and join Helen."

Alvin blinked at the cookie in his hand, obviously flustered. "Someone had to do it," he mumbled.

"Well, maybe Helen's seen the light," Courtenay suggested. "She knew what would happen if she ignored Claire's warning today, and she went ahead and did it. Maybe the Spirit Club doesn't mean as much to her as we thought."

Delaney shook her head. "I'm sure it still does, so Helen was really standing up for herself when she walked out on that field. I just wish she had a date for the dance this Saturday night. It would mean so much if she could be there."

"What do you mean, you wish Helen had a date?" Pammi asked. "How about Courtenay and me? We're not exactly inundated with invitations, you know."

"Oh, I think I can guess who your dream dates will be."

Delaney smiled at her best friends, feeling ridiculously lighthearted. This was the best part of organizing a dance, the matchmaking end of it. This is why she wanted to become a full-fledged cupid, so she could spend endless hours figuring out which boy was best suited for which girl, and vice versa. And then she could go ahead with fixing up the perfect couples and enjoying the romantic consequences.

Beside her Alvin groaned and rolled his eyes heavenward. "Don't get her started playing cupid. You don't know what you're in for."

Delaney poked him good-naturedly in the ribs while the others giggled, but inwardly the words hit home. Playing cupid. She had five days left. One short week of inhabiting a teenager's body and a teenager's mind and Saturday night, the eve of the dance, it would all change. Good-bye forever, high school days. Good-bye to teasing Alvin and sharing secrets with her close friends and trying on dresses at Tatters. Would she be able to leave Woodside High School when the time came? It was going to be incredibly difficult. She stared around the table at the three people closest to her and grinned goofily, trying to hide the tears that unexpectedly pricked her eyes. That was the thing about human beings: They cried at all the emotional moments, whereas cupids only cry over thwarted love relationships.

"Hey, hey, hey, reinforcements are here," Pammi announced, with a sideways grin at Courtenay.

Delaney turned to see Mitch, Tim, and John enter Le Scoop. The boys laughingly crammed into the back booth and teased the girls about their junk food diet. Mitch had slid in next to a pink-cheeked Courtenay and was trying to steal bites of her brownie. Tim sat across from Pammi and eyed her from beneath those perfectly straight eyebrows of his. For once Pammi refrained from making sarcastic remarks or jokes at Tim's expense. It looked like the cold war between the two was really over.

Yes, Delaney sighed contentedly, it just might work out after all. The hearts-and-flowers dance, her friends finding their Mr. Rights, and, best of all, a successful mission to earn her cupid wings and fly up. She peered over at Alvin and sighed again, this time in frustration. If only she could leave Woodside High knowing Alvin would find happiness and romance in his senior year. It would take a special girl to see through the shy, scholarly side of Alvin and discover all his wonderful, caring traits. But which girl among all the many at school?

"I've got good news for you," John said, breaking into her reflective thoughts. The yearbook editor reached into his pocket and pulled out a piece of paper, which he waggled playfully in front of her face. "Get a look at this."

"How can she when you keep whipping it around?" Pammi demanded. "You're making her dizzy."

John stuck out his tongue at Pammi but obediently put the mysterious item into Delaney's hands. Delaney scanned the paper with a puzzled frown.

"I don't get it, John. What is it? It's just a lot of names to me, some I know, some I don't know."

"That list, for your information, happens to be all the kids who asked to help organize the dance. I decided it would be a good idea to get some volunteers."

Delaney stared down at the list, eyes widening. "All these kids? Why, there must be fifty or sixty names on here."

"Let me see." Pammi took the sheet and let out a low whistle. "This is fantastic! Talk about a workforce . . . And even better, Delaney, I see a lot of seniors on this list."

"Really?"

"No kidding. That protest of ours must have done the trick, all right. We're actually getting seniors coming out from beneath the all-powerful thumb of Claire Reggio."

"She must be furious enough as it is to lose her Mogul

Madness prom," Courtenay said, "without realizing she's losing control over half the senior class to our dance."

"I don't know about half," John said, "but at least we've made a start. And I think what we should do is schedule a meeting for all those volunteers, the sooner the better, so they don't lose interest."

"Good idea," Delaney agreed. "Maybe we can post a notice or have the P.A. crew announce a volunteer get-together for, what? Tuesday at noon by the fountain? After school? What's best?"

"Lunchtime," Tim suggested. "That way we catch them at school. After school they'll have too many excuses and reasons to cut out."

"The slave driver knows," Pammi offered, but immediately added, "Just teasing," with a mischievous smile at Tim. Tim actually smiled back.

Delaney took a sip of the ice cream soda, then regretfully pushed it away. "Let's discuss what we'll need to do at the meeting tomorrow. I have some ideas."

For the next half hour they selected a theme ("A Valentine Ball is perfect," everyone agreed, "it's closest in spirit to the Dream Prom idea"); invitees ("Let's open it up to the whole school, all four classes; we'll get more kids and make more money," suggested Tim); and events for the dance ("Let's have contests and prizes," Delaney offered, "like for Most Romantic Costumes, Most Romantic Couple, Most Romantic Dancing . . ." "There she goes, Miss Romantic," Pammi teased). The seven were in perfect agreement until the topic of entertainment came up. Then everyone had his or her own idea and wouldn't budge. Pammi wanted to hire a deejay to play his own tapes; Mitch wouldn't hear of canned music, insisted on a live band—preferably his. Courtenay knew of a local group of musicians who played big-band 40's songs, and John gagged and said he wouldn't be caught dead dancing to that old-fashioned, boring music. "Well, we're going to need something different to bring in the kids," Courtenay said defensively. On and on it went, with tempers fraying and no one able to agree.

A bumblebee hiding over the noisy table suddenly stirred into action. He crawled up the sides of the restaurant's radio and danced across the dial. As if by magic, the easy-listening station playing light rock switched to the top 40 hit "Dream Only of Me." Listening to Storm Devrie's voice fill the tiny dessert shop, the bumblebee almost smiled, then edged cautiously along the woodwork until he reached a spot where he could observe Cupid Delaney and her friends.

Delaney had been refereeing the argument, but stopped the minute the song began to register. " 'Dream Only of Me,' " she murmured in a dazed voice. Storm Devrie's ballad jolted her with the force of an electrical charge. That's it, Delaney thought, sitting upright. That's the perfect choice for our entertainment. We're all going crazy trying to find second-rate imitators and inexpensive bands, but Storm Devrie would be the perfect entertainment for the Valentine Ball.

"Hey, listen, you guys, what if we—" Delaney began, but the words faded under the collective gaze of her friends.

Listen to me, she thought. I must be crazy. Or dreaming, like the song says. Why would a major recording artist and teen soap star agree to perform at a local high school's dinky Valentine Ball?

"What if we—what?" Mitch asked.

"Come on, Delaney, don't keep us hanging," Pammi said.

"Oh, nothing, that is . . ." She stared at them helplessly,

too embarrassed to even voice her brainstorm about Storm, when she felt a tap on her shoulder.

"Excuse me," a voice said behind her, "is this your paper? It was on the floor behind the booth."

She turned her head to see a newspaper thrust in her face, a white-jacketed waiter or busboy offering it to her. But not any waiter. It was the mysterious blond-haired boy who kept popping up at the strangest moments and disappearing again. Here he was, bright eyes sparkling, handsome face beaming down at hers, whole body practically humming with energy.

She sucked in her breath and stared at him. When she didn't move, he laughed and placed the paper in her frozen hands. Blinking in confusion, she looked down at the newspaper ("Sunday's entertainment pages," she mumbled) and then up again. But he was gone, as she suspected. He had somehow managed to slip away, on a break, perhaps, or had been called into the kitchen. He was a master of the Houdini escape.

"Delaney, what is it?" Mitch asked. "You look funny."

"Did you see him? The waiter who handed me the paper?"

Pammi gave a low wolf whistle. "You mean the dark-haired hunk with the glasses? Wow."

"What do you mean, glasses?" Courtenay objected. "He wasn't wearing glasses!"

"The guy had hair the color of Alvin's," Tim said. "That isn't dark to me."

"You're out of your mind," John protested. "He had no hair; he was practically bald."

They were arguing heatedly. Delaney threw up her hands in irritation and let them go at it. If this was their idea of a joke, it certainly wasn't funny. She began thumbing through the listings of New York and northern New

Jersey theater, movies, and local events. Suddenly, an item way down at the very bottom of the page caught her eye. The words *Young Dreamers* leaped out at her. As though hypnotized, she read through the short piece once, then read it more carefully a second time just to make sure she got the facts straight.

"I don't mean to interrupt the argument," she began, fighting to keep her voice steady, "but I want to read you something, if I may."

Pammi looked across at Delaney, eyebrows raised. "You know, Mitch is right. You *do* look strange. What's going on?"

Delaney rustled the paper. "Just listen. Headline: 'Real Life Rocker Goes to Bat.' Story: 'Soap star Storm Devrie has been flying to radio stations around the country to promote his "Dream Only of Me" single from the recently platinum album, "Storm's On the Way." On Monday, May twenty-first, the actor-singer will join "Young Dreamers" co-stars and some ten stars from such soaps as "General Hospital" and "All My Children" in a softball game to benefit the homeless at Oakdale City College stadium.' "

"Storm Devrie in Oakdale?" Pammi exclaimed incredulously. "Oakdale, New Jersey? That's only ten minutes away!"

"Oh, Delaney, is it true?" Courtenay leaned across the table, Mitch and the remains of the brownie totally forgotten.

"Who is this soap guy Storm whatever his name is," Tim asked, "and why all the hoopla?"

Alvin grinned and threw up his hands. "Don't ask. Don't even think about asking. All females are literally gaga about him—especially Delaney, Pammi, and Courtenay."

The three girls exchanged secret, electric glances.

106

"Oakdale . . ." whispered Courtenay.

"Just one town over," said Delaney, "and Pammi's got her car."

"What time does the softball game start?" Pammi asked.

Delaney rechecked the paper. "Four o'clock."

The girls looked up at the wall clock simultaneously, then at each other.

"It's three-fifty-three," announced Delaney.

A lengthy pause followed that was dramatically broken when Pammi jumped up. "Well, what are we sitting around here for? Let's move!"

"Uh, sorry, guys, but this is something we've got to do," Delaney explained with an apologetic smile as she slid out of the booth. "But we're all set for the meeting tomorrow, aren't we?"

"Well, yeah, I guess," Tim said, "but we never did figure out what the entertainment would be for the dance."

Delaney gave him an impish grin. "Let's just say 'mystery guest' and leave it at that for now, okay?"

"Mystery guest," repeated Tim in a puzzled voice.

The four boys raised their eyebrows and stared at Delaney. She stared back at them, then turned on her heel and spun out of the dessert shop, Pammi and Courtenay following.

"Mystery guest," Mitch and John said together.

Alvin bit into the cookie and grinned. "Hey, take it from one who knows. Don't ask. Just don't ask."

# Seeing Stars of the Softball Kind

They had one stop to make on the way to Oakdale.

"We've got to find Helen and take her with us," Delaney said as they pulled out of the mall parking lot. "After all, she's a charter member of the Saturday Night Dream Club. She'd hate it if she missed the chance to see Storm Devrie in the flesh."

But Helen wasn't at home.

"She's at the library, of course," Helen's sister told them at the door. "Where else would she be?"

"We've got to do something about Helen's social life," Delaney vowed a few minutes later as they parked in front of the town library. "And the very first thing is to wean her away from this place. You heard her sister's comment just now."

Pammi quirked an eyebrow in Delaney's direction. "Sounds like someone else we all know."

"You can't mean me," Delaney sputtered.

"No, silly, you're the biggest party planner and social butterfly around. I'm talking about Alvin."

"Oh."

"Yes, oh. Or haven't you noticed? It's almost like he and Helen are identical twins when it comes to their time clocked in libraries and study hall."

"There's not a thing wrong with getting good grades," Delaney protested with a smile. The comment about Helen and Alvin made her pause, got her brainwaves spinning. Helen and Alvin. They had once been a close duo, before Helen lost her heart (and her senses) to Craig Lacrosse. When would Helen wake up to the fact that Craig Lacrosse was not worth one eighth of an Alvin Danziger?

"Are you listening to me or daydreaming again?" Pammi asked. "Is our local cupid off in another hemisphere?"

"What!" Delancy's jaw dropped open, but she managed a weak laugh when she realized her friend was teasing. "Oh, yeah, sure. Just call me cupid, all right. Listen, Pammi, you and Courtenay wait here while I run in and find Helen."

Delaney scrambled from the car. Courtenay poked her head out of the backseat window. "Well, don't be too long. It's already four o'clock!"

Helen was by the second-floor card catalog when Delaney found her, but she wasn't alone. Claire and Craig were sitting nearby at a table, heads bent together, giggling. Well, well, the king and queen of Woodside High actually gracing the library with their presence, Delaney thought as she hurriedly greeted Helen. That's a shock.

"Helen, put aside whatever you're doing and come with me right now," Delaney said. "Pammi and Courtenay are waiting for us in the car."

Helen's eyes shifted nervously across to Claire and Craig, who had stopped whispering to listen to the conversation. "Well, ah, I can't. I'm helping Craig with—I mean, I'm adding footnotes to that Conrad paper."

Delaney gripped Helen's shoulders. "Forget Joseph Conrad and forget the footnotes. This is more important."

"But—"

Delaney whispered into Helen's ear. When she finished, Helen stood motionless, as if not believing what she had just heard.

Claire nudged Craig and said in a clear voice, "Don't worry. Your private researcher isn't going anywhere."

Helen blinked and came to her senses. She slammed the catalog drawer shut and hurled her note cards on the table in front of the two seniors.

"Let's go," she said to Delaney.

"Hey! Wait one second!" Craig shot up from his seat, disbelief splashed all over his face. "You can't just leave without doing those footnotes. I won't pass unless I have the footnotes on the paper."

Helen kept on walking.

Now Claire rose. "I hope you know what this means, Helen. I was willing to ignore your protest this morning on the playing field, but this is inexcusable. If you take one more step, you're out of the Spirit Club."

Helen paused, seemed to struggle within herself, then faced Claire.

"I can't be kicked out of your club, remember? It's one of the rules you made up yourself." Turning on her heel, she walked out the door, a jubilant Delaney beside her.

"Hey, wait!" Craig called, a note of pleading in his voice. "Helen? I'll pay you to do the footnotes. Whatever you want. Helen . . .?"

He glowered at Claire, who sank into her chair and glowered back.

The plump bumblebee who had sailed into the library

with Delaney now gleefully executed a loop-the-loop around the two annoyed seniors before soaring out the front door with Helen and Delaney. He flew into Delaney's large tote bag when her head was turned, burrowing deep into the lip glosses and eyeliner brushes of a plastic makeup kit.

The game was well into the third inning by the time the four girls bought their tickets at the gate and found seats high in the stands overlooking left field. The stadium was packed with screaming, cheering soap opera fans. Whenever an actor came up to bat, the spectators went wild, calling out his or her name and waving hand-lettered signs and banners.

"And I thought Mets games were crazy," Courtenay observed.

"Do you see Storm?" Helen asked. She clutched Delaney's arm. "Where's Storm?"

They eagerly scanned the field, failed to find him, and peered across at the dugout.

"There!" Delaney pointed, half rising in excitement. "He's sitting between Mark Hall and Chad Collier on the bench! In the turquoise shirt and white jeans."

Pammi followed Delaney's finger and frowned. "That tiny little stick figure the size of an ant is Storm Devrie? How can you even tell from way up here? We're so far away we'll never get a chance to ask him for an autograph, let alone see his gorgeous face."

"Well, I don't care." Helen sighed, smiling blissfully. "Just to know we're in the same ball park is a miracle."

"Ooh, look!" an older woman behind the girls shrieked. "Storm Devrie's up at bat next! And the bases are loaded!"

"Who's winning?" Pammi turned and asked the woman.

"With Storm Devrie playing, who cares?" she replied.

"There's a woman after my own heart," Courtenay quipped.

"Storm, we love you!" girls two rows down squealed.

Over the loudspeaker Storm Devrie's name and soap opera were announced to tumultuous applause. The handsome actor waved to his fans, then approached the mound, bat in hand.

"I'd give anything to be that bat right now," Pammi said with a sigh.

"You are," Courtenay told her. "You're batty."

Pammi rolled her eyes, then jumped up with a cry. "Oh, no, strike one!"

"Come on, Storm!" The older woman behind them screamed. "We need a hit!"

The actor paused, raised the bat, swung, and missed. "Strike two!"

"Oh, I can't look!" Helen shut her eyes. "I don't want to see him strike out!"

While the four girls held their breaths, edged forward in their seats . . .

. . . *Andrew hastily extricated himself from the makeup case and zoomed toward the baseball diamond in record time.*

*I wish the mighty Storm Devrie would strike out, he said under his breath, his bumblebee face tightening a little. It might do wonders for his ego, which is probably the size of Texas. Honestly, Andrew grumbled to himself, what's so all-fired good-looking about that guy anyway? What is it that turned all these thousands of females, Cupid Delaney included, into a bowl of mush and has them screaming his name? Andrew couldn't figure it out as he hovered over home plate.*

*Still, he wanted to help Cupid Delaney. He knew what she yearned for, what she dreamed for her Valentine Ball. And if he could use his powers, however wrongly or illegally, he'd do it. He had to admit, though, it really irked him that such a sensitive, clever Love Bureau trainee as Cupid Delaney was so moony-eyed over this Storm creature.*

*The soap star gritted his teeth and faced the pitcher once more. Andrew sprinkled some invisible celestial dust over Storm Devrie's bat and said the magic words. As if in slow motion, the ball spun out of the pitcher's hand and connected with the actor's bat like a powerful magnet. Storm grunted at the impact and swung hard.*

*I must be out of my mind, Andrew cried as he jumped on the ball at the very last second before it soared high in the air. Hanging on for dear life, he steered the home-run ball so that it sailed in a direct line to the left-field balcony seats . . . curving away from the hundreds of hands that reached up to grab for it, spinning in its course until it reached the dazed and unsuspecting figure of Cupid Delaney, who had taken her eyes off the game to read her program.*

*Oh, no! Andrew gasped, realizing too late that he couldn't land the ball as delicately as he hoped.*

*"Delaney, watch out!" Pammi thrust out her hands to protect her friend, but the ball zipped past her fingers to clip a startled Cupid Delaney right on the crown of her blonde head.*

*Andrew jumped off the ball to check on Cupid Delaney's condition, buzzing anxiously in front of her face. She put a hand to her forehead, wobbled unceremoniously on rubber legs, and said, "Am I seeing stars or are those bumblebees?" before collapsing into her seat.*

*Sorry, Cupid, Andrew mentally apologized, but I had to do it. And you'll thank me for it on Saturday night!*

When Delaney came to, the most incredible vision was floating before her dazed eyes. It couldn't be, she thought, struggling to sit up and failing, but *it looks like Storm Devrie peering down at me. And he's even more gorgeous* in real life than on TV, with crisp black hair, Malibu blue eyes, and that incredibly vulnerable smile.

"Hey," the fantasy man said with genuine concern, "are you all right?"

The vision talked! She must be hallucinating from that knock on her head. She gazed into her fantasy's eyes and broke into a silly smile.

"Oh, Storm, we're the most loyal fan club you've got. We're the Saturday Night Dream Club and we're using your song for our theme at the dance Saturday night and all the kids at school love it, too, but Pammi, Courtenay, Helen and I love it the best . . ." She was babbling away, until the vision burst into relieved laughter and turned away to address someone else.

"I guess she's all right," Storm said. "She talking a mile a minute."

Delaney peered up in shock to see a woman's face close to Storm's. How did a total stranger get into her personal fantasy? The woman smiled down at Delaney and took her hand.

"Her pulse is a little high," the woman remarked to Storm, "but maybe that has more to do with your presence than the slight blow she took to her head. I'm sure she's fine."

It was no fantasy! Storm Devrie was actually hovering solicitously over her, Storm the man, not Storm the daydream. And a doctor had just examined her. Delaney struggled to sit up, and instantly she felt his arms around her, helping her. Staring disbelieving at her were Pammi, Courtenay, and Helen, not to mention the spectators, who watched this entire incident with open mouths.

"Are you *sure* you're all right?" Storm demanded. "You know, I feel personally responsible for what's happened to you."

Delaney drank in his face, his warm concern, the reality of his presence. Tongue-tied, she could only stare helplessly at the young actor and singer whom she had idolized for months. Beside her a bumblebee had crawled out from beneath her seat and paced in mounting irritation at her inability to function because of her proximity to Storm. The bee buzzed in warning fashion when the soap star reached down and took Delaney's hand.

"Oh," Delaney gasped, cheeks turning bright pink. Her heart began pounding so loudly she thought everyone could hear it.

"You're a strange girl, you know that?" Storm squeezed her fingers and grinned at her. The bee began hopping up and down in a tribal war dance. "Are you sure there isn't anything I can do to make up for this horrible accident? Please. I want to do something, especially for such a loyal fan."

Delaney thought furiously for a few seconds and made up her mind.

"Well, there *is* one thing . . ."

She crooked her finger, and Storm obligingly leaned close enough for her to whisper in his ear. He listened intently, nodding his head when she finished. He had just announced, "It's a deal; let's seal it with a kiss," and had begun to pucker up when he yelped and jumped high in the air.

"Something stung me!" he howled. "Something stung me!"

The bumblebee smirked and began to hum a completely different tune as he hurriedly took off.

# So Close to Success

The Sweetheart Squad leaders were bored. They had been ordered to monitor another cupid's assignment in Arizona, and for two days had stayed glued to the trainee's every move.

"This is the dullest mission I've ever seen," Enchantée complained, not even bothering to stifle a yawn. "If I ever see another cactus, I'll scream."

"This is the dullest cupid," Bella Rosa agreed. "She does everything by the book and never once flaunts the rules. She's so letter-perfect it's a bore, bore, BORE!"

"You know the mission's going to work out without a hitch," Passionata added. "So where's the mystery? Where's the suspense?"

"Where's the excitement that's always alive and present in Cupid Delaney's fiascos?" Bella Rosa said.

"Speaking of our feisty cupid, I wonder how she's doing?"

Bella Rosa shot Enchantée a warning look. "Don't even think of it. Don't even play with the notion of changing channels. You know we've been ordered to monitor Cupid Alyssa's mission nonstop until Thursday."

"But Cupid Alyssa is so incredibly perfect she's driving me insane. And besides, didn't you hear what happened to Cupid Delaney at the Oakdale stadium? There was a charity softball *game between soap opera actors and Storm Devrie's home-run ball hit Cupid Delaney in the head and he came up into the stands to talk to her and apologize."*

*"He never!"*

*"He did. Isn't this better than a TV soap?"*

*"So what happened?" Bella Rosa demanded, obviously no longer bored.*

*Enchantée slyly grinned and pointed to the screen. "Why not tune in to the continuing saga of Cupid Delaney and find out for yourself?"*

*"Come on, Bella Rosa," urged Passionata. "I'm dying to know! And the Woodside dance is only three days away."*

*Defenses crumbling, the dark-haired demigoddess bit her lip, but finally nodded. Cheering, Enchantée flipped channels and focused in on a bright-eyed Cupid Delaney. She was surrounded by a group of her friends in Mrs. Argon's outer office, selling tickets to a line of students so long it snaked all the way down the hallway and into the stairwell.*

*The Senior Sweetheart members gaped first at the screen, then at each other.*

*"I can't believe my eyes," Enchantée cried. "Are all those teenagers actually buying tickets for Cupid Delaney's dance?"*

*"How did she ever manage to turn the school's attitude around? Focus in on what she's passing out with the ticket," Bella Rosa asked Enchantée. The screen zoomed to a close-up of the object in Cupid Delaney's hand. It was a Valentine-red paper badge that boldly stated* We Got Heart. *The cupid trainee helped the girl who had just purchased a ticket to the Valentine Ball pin it to her top.*

*"We got heart," Bella Rosa murmured with a delighted grin. "If that isn't just like our Cupid Delaney. She really is too much."*

*"I'd say things were looking up for our little rebel," Enchantée*

117

declared. "And high time, too. If she fails this mission, it's bye-bye Love Bureau for sure."

"Where's Andrew? Knowing him, he should be buzzing somewhere close to our cupid. I bet he's relieved the mission's going so well."

They searched through Mrs. Argon's office until they spotted him, a fat bumblebee peeking out from beneath the advance-sale ticket table at an animated Cupid Delaney.

"There he is," Bella Rosa giggled. "As closely attached to our cupid trainee as ever."

"Maybe too attached?" Enchantée frowned, fine-tuned the picture of the bee. "Look at the expression in Andrew's eyes and tell me what you think. I hope I'm wrong, but . . ."

Passionata and Bella Rosa shot Enchantée perplexed looks, but obeyed her command. There was silence in the viewing room while the demigoddesses studied the bee, and then Bella Rosa sat back, uttering a celestial curse.

"Jumping Jupiter, Enchantée, you're right. You're absolutely right."

Passionata groaned. "Why did that impressionable fool of a male cupid have to lose his objectivity so thoroughly? You can see feelings for Cupid Delaney written all over those bumblebee features of his."

"He'd better not do anything to risk our trainee's chances of succeeding in her mission. If Valentina found out—oh, I don't even like to imagine what she'd do."

"She'd yank him off the case immediately," Enchantée said. "And cancel the assignment. And who knows if she'd give Cupid Delaney another chance?"

"But it wouldn't be fair. It's not Cupid Delaney's fault if Andrew's flipped head over wings for her."

Enchantée gave a short, cynical laugh. "Tell that to our no-nonsense Love Bureau administrator. No, on second thought, tell Valentina nothing. She can't find out about Andrew's feelings for

118

*Cupid Delaney, not one word, not one hint. And, Bella Rosa, this particularly means you."*

*"Me?" The Sweetheart member was indignant.*

*"Yes, you're well meaning, but you cannot keep a secret to save your life. Well, if you want Cupid Delaney's Valentine Ball to go off without any problems, and have her earn her wings, you can't blurt out the news about our bumblebee to Valentina, or to anyone."*

*The three demigoddesses heard Valentina's distinctive voice in the corridor and froze.*

*"Quick, switch back to the cactus-and-desert assignment," Bella Rosa urged.*

*Enchantée changed the channel just as Valentina poked her head into the monitoring room. "And how's everything going in here?" she demanded.*

*"Oh, ah, fine, perfect, everything couldn't be better," Passionata sang out.*

*But the tension in the room belied the confident statement.*

*"Andrew," Enchantée whispered after Valentina left, "don't you dare do anything foolish to ruin Cupid's mission. I know you mean well and you probably want to help, but be careful! She's never come this close before!"*

Down below, Delaney was unconsciously echoing Enchantée's sentiments.

I've never gotten this close to earning my wings, Delaney thought, selling student after student tickets to the dance. And this time I have Storm Devrie to thank for the success of the dance. Wasn't he the reason for the overwhelming demand for Valentine Ball tickets? Once the kids found out who the mystery guest would be, there was no stopping them.

I still can't believe my luck, Delaney thought, replaying once again in her mind the fantastic scene of Storm hovering over her, holding her hand, telling her he'd do anything to make up for the accident. Well, she had asked him a favor and he had agreed. The current number one recording star in America was going to appear at Woodside High this coming Saturday night to perform his hit single and several other songs from his best-selling album. He had even suggested that he judge the Most Romantic contests. It had all been too exciting to be true, but it was true. Three days from now the gym would be transformed into a magical wonderland of dreams and romance. And the school would have the best Valentine Ball ever.

"I'm going to make it, Valentina," Delaney whispered. "You wait and see."

"Excuse me, Delaney, did you say something?" Mrs. Argon asked, coming up behind her.

"Oh, ah, no, I mean, yes. I said, we're going to make it, wait and see. I mean, make the dance a sellout."

The senior advisor beamed. "The way ticket sales are going, I'd say you have no problem with that prediction. In fact, you may want to print more tickets before they disappear completely. After all, you'll need to sell some at the door, won't you?"

"I never thought of that." Delaney turned to Courtenay and Helen, who were in charge of handling the money for the sales. "I hate to leave you guys in the lurch, but I need to sneak out and find Tim to ask him about printing more tickets before we run out. Will you be all right until Todd and LuAnne relieve you?"

Courtenay made shooing noises. "Go, girl, go. Helen and I can handle the mob scene without you."

"Thanks, you're both terrific," said Delaney as she hurried out the door. In the midst of all the noise and chatter coming from the ticket line, she never heard the hum of the bumblebee that followed her out of the office and into the crowded hall. Kids greeted her on the way to the journalism department, flashing their heart badges proudly. Ever since her prom campaign started a week and a half ago, she had become a familiar face to most of the school. And the protest on Monday and subsequent meeting with the principal had only added to her fame. "Look out," one of her classmates teased as she hurried past, "there goes the Wicked Picket Lady!"

Delaney laughed as she turned the corner and entered the outer office of the journalism department.

"Hi, Mrs. Deltorro," she greeted the department assistant, "is Tim around?"

"He's here, but he's in the conference room and I'm afraid he can't be disturbed. The *Bulletin* staff and teaching advisors are voting for next year's editorial slate."

"Is it all right if I wait out here until they're finished?"

"Be my guest. They should be wrapping it up in a few minutes."

Delaney perched on one of the reception chairs, but then noticed a group of students whispering and giggling and poring over something by a large table in the corner. Curious and too full of energy to sit still, she went over to investigate.

"What's going on?"

One of the girls, a classmate from English lit, pointed to an avalanche of proof sheets and individual 3-inch by 5-inch head shots.

"We're sorting and putting names to class photographs for the yearbook. The photographer got them back to us this morning, and we have to alphabetize them."

"Wow. Is this every single student at Woodside?"

"Juniors and seniors on the right side, and underclassmen on the left. Why, want to help?"

"Better not. I'd probably get in your way." But then a

funny thought popped into her head. The photograph of every single student in Woodside High was on the table before her. Therefore, it logically followed that the ever-appearing and disappearing blond boy was in this massive pile. Somewhere, perhaps right under her very nose, was the name of the handsome Houdini who baffled and intrigued her.

Pushing right up to the table, Delaney went straight to work. She studied proof sheet after proof sheet of the junior and senior classes, but couldn't find the boy. Delaney couldn't believe it. Where was her rescuer? If he attended the school, he had to be here. *Had to be.*

"I don't get it," she murmured. "Where are you? *What* are you?"

Determinedly, growing more hyper and crazy by the minute, she pored over every individual photograph, every single proof sheet before her. Lurking by the open window in the office, a bumblebee seemed to be enjoying her disconcerted state of mind.

"I'm not giving up," Delaney muttered, setting her jaw. "Not until I find you. And you're close. I can feel it."

Once or twice she'd stop in a burst of excitement, believing she'd found a photo of the mysterious boy. But upon closer examination, the features weren't the same, the expression different. Faster and faster she tore through the pile until only one proof sheet remained. She studied it minutely, holding her breath, then tossed it aside angrily.

"Are you sure this is everything the photographer sent?" Delaney snapped. She couldn't believe it, but he had done it again; the blond boy had slipped right through her fingers.

"Sorry," her friend said, "but this is it. Hey, are you okay? You look like King Kong did when he lost the girl."

"You know something, Karen? I *feel* like King Kong," Delaney agreed with a rueful smile. Only it wasn't the girl she had lost, but the boy. She pushed away from the table and went to the window. With vacant eyes, she stared out at the quad, absentmindedly playing with the blind cord. A bumblebee froze on the edge of the window, directly in Delaney's line of vision. But she looked straight through the black and yellow creature, immersed in her own confusing thoughts.

What's the matter with me? she worried. Why do I feel so upset over not finding this boy? What does it matter who he is? I'm dating Alvin. He's my boyfriend. This other boy means nothing. Absolutely nothing.

Then why was her mind whirling with images of the boy's face, the unusually colored eyes that always gazed at her so warmly, the crooked grin? Why did she feel so empty inside because she couldn't find him? What was happening to her anyway, and why did she care so much?

And then she forgot all these thoughts as the door to the conference room burst open and a distraught Pammi raced out.

"Pammi," Delaney cried, hurrying over to her. "What's wrong?"

Pammi's eyes were blurred by tears. "I didn't get feature articles editor. I thought I was the best qualified, I really did, but they chose Jennifer Hardy instead."

Delaney put a consoling arm around her friend's trembling shoulders.

"I'm sorry, Pammi. I know how much you wanted that position."

"It isn't even that as much as knowing that Tim didn't vote for me. Can you believe it, Delaney? I thought he would; he told me I've been doing a great job on the paper, and he turns around and picks Jennifer instead."

The object of their discussion rushed out of the conference room at that moment, stopping short when he spotted Pammi.

"Well, for Pete's sake, why did you leave the meeting
before it was over? Come back inside."

Pammi straightened and hurriedly brushed away her
tears. "Why should I bother?"

"Why bother? Because they're announcing the position
of assistant editor next, and I definitely think you should
be there."

"You can't mean . . . Are you saying . . .?"

Tim's normally serious eyes glinted in amused affec-
tion. "I'm saying that Pamela Gittner better get her act
together and make it into the conference room to receive
her new position before the committee decides to go over
my head and select someone else."

Pammi's crestfallen face lit up. She stared at Tim in
joyful disbelief.

"I got it? I made assistant editor? Oh, Tim, I'm so
happy! I'm so happy! Thanks for recommending me!"

Tim looked flushed and inordinately pleased. "You were
the best candidate we had. Of course, I may have been a
little biased. And I think you should know that being
assistant editor means you'll have to go to the Valentine
Ball with the current editor, just part of the job require-
ment," he said, searching Pammi's eyes.

Pammi laughed, then impulsively leaned over to kiss
Tim.

"That's an offer I can't refuse," she said. With a backward wink and glowing smile for Delaney, she returned
to the conference room with Tim.

Ah, true love, Delaney sighed. How could I have interrupted that magic moment to ask Tim a mundane ques-

tion about tickets for the dance? I'll have to catch him later, after they've both come down from cloud nine.

Smiling, Delaney left the office just as Claire and Dawn swept by, surrounded as usual by the Spirit Club fan club. Delaney trailed unnoticed in their wake, feeling a little like a rowboat following a mighty ocean liner. Waves of kids parted in Claire's path. Delaney hadn't consciously been listening to Claire's conversation until she heard her name pop up, but then she was all ears, creeping closer to the entourage.

". . . Delaney's Valentine Ball, are you?" someone asked Claire.

Claire stopped abruptly, creating a traffic jam in the middle of the hall. "*Of course* I'm going to the dance Saturday night. I wouldn't miss it for the world. It's going to be the best entertainment this school has ever had."

Delaney couldn't believe her ears. Was this really Claire Reggio talking, her nemesis and arch enemy and sworn opponent to sentimental social events? But then Claire continued. "I'm going and I urge all of you to buy tickets, but I'm only going to be there for one thing: to witness the disaster it's going to be."

"But Storm Devrie's going to be there," someone piped up nervously.

Claire snorted. "She *says* Storm Devrie's going to show, but you know something? I don't believe it. I don't believe it for one moment. No major TV star and number one rock singer is going to waste his time appearing at a podunk school like Woodside when he's not being paid. I know the entertainment industry, and I can assure you, he may have told Delaney he'd make an appearance, but he's probably forgotten all about it by now. No way is Storm Devrie going to be at the dance Saturday night, and I wouldn't miss seeing Delaney fall flat on her face for anything."

Claire and her friends laughed and the group moved on. But Delaney remained, standing motionless in the hall. Of course Storm Devrie was going to appear at Woodside High Saturday night. He'd sing his smash hit, "Dream Only of Me," and make the Valentine Ball the most romance-filled evening the kids would ever experience. And she would earn her wings, succeed in her assignment, and fly up. Claire was just being her usual negative self by uttering that dire prediction.

"Oh, please," Delaney whispered, "I'm so close to becoming a cupid. Please don't let me fail now." She walked slowly back to the journalism department, head bowed, an agitated bumblebee circling behind her.

# Countdown to the Dance

Two days before the dance.

The kids at Woodside High were eagerly counting down, chattering excitedly about the outfits they'd be wearing and the dates they'd invited. Much of the talk revolved around Storm Devrie. Despite Claire's loudly voiced assertion that the soap star wouldn't show, tickets for the Valentine Ball were briskly selling. And Delaney had become the reigning heroine of the school.

During fifth period on Thursday, she, Alvin, and Helen perched on the ledge inside the quad, enjoying the warmth of the sun as they ate their lunches. Students walking by invariably greeted Delaney by pointing to their heart badges or congratulating her on the upcoming dance. Someone playing a radio turned the volume up when "Dream Only of Me" came on. Two girls sprawled nearby on the grass squealed when boys passing by mock formally invited them to dance and waltzed them around in time to the music. A feeling of springtime and romance was in the air.

Helen stared at the dancing couples with a wistful expression. She didn't say a word, but Delaney knew what she was thinking. Impulsively, looking across at an unsuspecting Alvin, Delaney made up her mind.

"Helen, Alvin wants to ask you something."

Alvin stopped struggling with the top of his fruit juice bottle and blinked at Delaney. The puppy-dog eyes behind the glasses were bewildered.

"I do?"

"Yes, you do." Delaney nodded firmly, eyes begging Alvin to play along. "Remember what you talked about, inviting Helen to go to the Valentine Ball with us?"

Alvin's face reddened. His mouth opened in shock. "I—I did?"

"He did?" Helen's voice came out in a squeak. She turned to Alvin. "You did? Really?" At once her face lit up with very real pleasure.

Delaney sat there, feeling like a spectator at a movie, while her two friends looked at each other in silence. Obviously both of them were shaken off balance by what they saw in each other's eyes and didn't know what to say.

Alvin recovered first. "Well, sure, of course. I want you to go to the dance with me, I mean, Delaney and me," he hastily corrected. "That is, if you don't already have a date."

Helen stared down at the ground and shook her head.

Alvin beamed. "Well, then, great. It's settled. You're going to the dance with me. Oh, and with Delaney, of course."

"Of course," Delaney repeated dryly, but smiled somewhat wistfully at Alvin. Honestly, what a big fool she had been. A complete idiot. Here she had been worrying about finding Alvin a perfect companion, and Helen Mapes had been that girl all along. They had similar interests and similar enthusiasms, and, best of all, feelings for each other that had never completely faded. Delaney stared at Helen and Alvin, who were exchanging pleased but embarrassed grins, and realized that things had come full circle from her first matchmaking adventure in November. Then she had to pull this couple apart to satisfy Valentina's wishes. Now she was letting nature (and love) work its own magic.

Delaney looked over at Alvin and sighed philosophically, not noticing the jubilant bumblebee who peeked up at her from underneath the ledge. Then Courtenay hurried over to them and flung herself angrily on the grass, startling the bee, who retreated even further under the ledge.

"You'll never guess what I just heard in the cafeteria," she stormed. "Not in a thousand, no, a million years! Oh, I am so mad I could scream!"

"This wouldn't have anything to do with a certain Mitch Rhyner, would it?" Delaney asked lightly.

"How did you know? Did you hear the gossip too?"

Delaney shrugged. "What else would make you so angry?"

Courtenay sat up. "Listen to this. I was standing in line in the cafeteria and in front of me were Anita Dayton and Susan Jerrard. And they were talking about the dance on Saturday night and figuring out who was taking whom. And then they brought up Mitch's name and they were disgusting, practically drooling when they talked about him, and Anita says, 'I wanted to ask him, but he's off limits now.' And Susan goes, 'Why? Is he dating someone?' And Anita leans over to whisper in Susan's ear so I had to turn a somersault over my tray to hear and she says: 'Don't you know? My cousin Rob plays in Mitch's band and he says Mitch is crazy about some girl, but he doesn't say who she is, only that she's pretty special.' And Susan says, 'She must be special if a hunk like Mitch goes for her.' And I couldn't stand to hear any more, I really couldn't, so I left."

Helen peeked over at Courtenay with a confused frown on her face.

"But why are you angry? You know that lots of girls have crushes on Mitch. And you're always saying that you don't like him."

"Well, I've changed my mind," Courtenay burst out. "I've fallen for Mitch and I thought he liked me, but now I find out he's dating someone else."

"But you don't know that for a fact," Delaney interjected. "That could just be gossip."

"I know, but then why hasn't he invited me to the Valentine Ball?"

Her unhappy question was left unanswered when the object of their discussion ambled into view.

"Oh, no," Courtenay whispered as Mitch walked over. She tried to get up, but Delaney kept a restraining hand on her shoulder.

"Hi, there," Mitch greeted them all with a friendly grin but reserved a special wink for Courtenay. Courtenay didn't return the smile. She stared at him without expression.

Giving Courtenay a puzzled glance, Mitch turned to Delaney. "Just wanted to check with you about Saturday night. You asked me about having my band play as backup for Storm, and I talked to the guys and they're all set. But there's just one matter I have to settle now before it's a go. And it involves Courtenay."

She looked up at him in surprise. "Me?"

Mitch cleared his throat nervously. "Keith can't play keyboards Saturday night, and I didn't want to try and find anyone else before I talked to you—hey! What's the matter?"

Courtenay had scrambled to her feet and was staring at Mitch, eyes blazing in indignation. "You're asking me to go to the Valentine Ball—as your *keyboard player?* Well, no. I'm sorry. I'm not available. Now if you'll excuse me, I have to go to my locker to get some books for French class." And with a backward glance at Delaney that said, "See? I told you so!" Courtenay flounced off.

Mitch's eyebrows shot up. "What is going on with that girl? She didn't even stick around long enough to find out what I wanted to say."

"I thought it was pretty obvious," Delaney said. "You wanted her to substitute for Keith on keyboards, right?"

"Wrong! I was going to ask Steve Banks, but I wasn't sure about his ability and I knew that Courtenay had played in the school symphony with him and could give me feedback on his style. What I wanted to ask Courtenay was something completely different, like if she'd be my date for the Valentine Ball, but I guess the answer's pretty obvious and—"

Delaney jumped off the ledge, interrupting him midstream. "What did you say? You want to take her to the dance?"

Mitch gave an embarrassed laugh. "Well, yes, but now she probably won't talk to me, let alone go to the dance with me."

Delaney smiled. "Don't you budge. Stay exactly where you are. I'm going to find that confused friend of mine and set her straight, and I want you to be here waiting if my words sink in."

"I'm not going anywhere," Mitch assured Delaney. "Not if you can fix things with Courtenay."

"There she goes again, playing cupid," said Alvin, throwing up his hands in mock despair. But his eyes crinkled with laughter, not criticism.

"That's one of Delaney's true talents," Helen said quietly, with an affectionate and thankful glance at her friend.

First with Pammi and Tim, then Helen and Alvin, and now hopefully with Courtenay and Mitch, Delaney had indeed played cupid and gotten her friends romantically paired. But that left Delaney the odd person out. And she couldn't very well break Love Bureau rules and cast a spell to produce the perfect boy for her own wilting love life. Stifling a sigh, she went in search of Courtenay and found her yanking books out of her locker in barely controlled fury. But a brief explanation about the mix-up with Mitch and the dance transformed the hurt and anger on Courtenay's face into happiness. Courtenay returned to the quad and to Mitch with a smile on her face.

At least I've worked some magic of my own with my best friends, Delaney reasoned proudly, watching Mitch swing Courtenay around. And that's nothing to sneer at. Lots of Love Bureau trainees can't even claim that. Now if only the Valentine Ball will go off as planned, she thought. It has to; otherwise, I'm out of the cupid business. And if I can't be a cupid, what am I going to do?

*Up in the elegant dining hall of the Love Bureau, Valentina and her Senior Sweetheart peers had just finished polishing off their midday meal of strawberries in cream and chocolate kisses. Valentina rose, dismissed the demigoddesses with a wave of her hand, but ordered Bella Rosa to stay. As Enchantée and Passionata left the room, they sent Bella Rosa warning looks that commanded her to keep their secret about Andrew.*

*Bella Rosa twisted her fingers in her lap and tried to act calm, but Valentina's first question made her jump.*

*"Have you seen Andrew at all today? He hasn't reported in."*

"Andrew?" Bella Rosa gulped and took a swallow of ice water to gain time.

Valentina arched an eyebrow. "Yes, Andrew. You remember him, don't you? As I recall, you and your friends have been following his assignment with Cupid Delaney quite closely."

"Uh, no, not that closely," Bella Rosa protested. "In fact, hardly at all since we discovered that he—" She clapped a hand over her mouth in dismay, but it was too late. Valentina pounced on her words like a shark gobbling down minnows.

"Yes, Bella Rosa, finish your statement. Since you discovered that he what? Something about Cupid Delaney? Something about the mission?"

"No! Yes! Oh, I can't tell!" cried Bella Rosa, shrinking under the goddess's piercing gaze. "I promised."

It took only a few minutes to extract the truth from a rattled Bella Rosa. Valentina digested the news of Andrew's attraction to Cupid Delaney in silence, staring off into space. Her face was grave and unsmiling.

"So," the Love Bureau administrator finally said, "we've got trouble."

Bella Rosa nervously popped chocolate kiss after chocolate kiss into her mouth. Finally she screwed up her courage. "Please don't blame Cupid Delaney, Valentina. She really hasn't done anything wrong."

"But can the same be said for our impetuous male cupid Andrew? What's he been up to? I think I need to find out."

She rose swiftly and snapped her fingers at Bella Rosa.

"Come with me. We have work to do."

Bella Rosa jumped up. "What kind of work?"

"Clear your calendar for the rest of the afternoon. You and I are going to be spending the day in the monitoring room, replaying the tapes of Cupid Delaney's mission. Only this time

*I'll be keeping an eye on the bumblebee, not the trainee. A very close eye."*

With a sinking heart, Bella Rosa followed the goddess out of the dining hall. Things didn't look good for Cupid Delaney. Things didn't look good at all.

# The Valentine Ball

Seven-thirty on Saturday night, the witching hour.

Delaney walked up to the open doors of the school gym and suddenly stopped short, unable to go in.

"Nervous?" asked Alvin, coming up behind her.

"Of course she is," Helen said, giving Delaney's arm a sympathetic squeeze. "Being in charge of a dance is pretty scary."

Delaney stared at the entrance in silence, sure the two could hear her heart thundering in her chest. As well meaning and supportive as Helen and Alvin were, they didn't have a clue in the world what she was going through, couldn't possibly know that her whole future would be decided that very night based on the success—or failure—of the Valentine Ball.

It's got to work, Delaney reassured herself. *It's just got to.*

But if it did, and this was the part she hated thinking about, it meant saying good-bye to all her friends and a wonderful way of life as a teenage girl. But you want to fly up, an inner voice whispered. You know you miss being a cupid. Of course I do, Delaney mentally retorted. But will I miss being a mortal even more?

No use debating the point anyway, not on the evening of the dance. Before she could break the spell and move, however, two things happened at once: A plump bumblebee flying overhead suddenly darted inside the gym doors just as Mitch and Courtenay and Tim and Pammi joined Delaney, Alvin, and Helen. The girls exchanged compliments and examined one another's hairstyles, dresses, and makeup.

"I'm dying to see how the gym looks!" Pammi exclaimed. "I hope our decorating committee does a better job with the Valentine theme than the sophomores did with that embarrassing Beach Blanket Under the Stars mixer last month. Ugh, I shudder when I think of it. And kids still can't get rid of the sand in their shoes."

Delaney hoped she looked more confident than she felt. "I stopped by this afternoon to see how the volunteers were doing and, well," she struggled for adjectives, "it was nice. Pleasant."

Courtenay made a face. "Nice? Pleasant? This from the most enthusiastic girl in school? I hate to be my usual pessimistic self, but it doesn't sound promising."

While Delaney and her friends were busy outside chatting . . .

. . . *Andrew was busy inside working.*

*And quite a lot to work on, too, he thought, grimly surveying the empty gym. Delaney had been right to be nervous. Kids coming to the Valentine Ball would be disappointed at the tacky and unromantic state of the decorations. Andrew darted about, correcting the most obvious flaws as best he could. The crudely drawn, cut-out cupids tacked to the walls . . . there! With a sprinkle of celestial confetti, the drawings became four-foot, three-dimensional creatures, almost glowing in pink-cheeked good health. And here, the red and white crepe paper streamers*

*dangling in a pathetic fashion from the basketball hoops . . . a*
*dash of magic dust, and ermine and ivory-colored satin and velvet*
*bands of ribbon twined together overhead to form a canopy fit for*
*a king. That ridiculous-looking net thrown over the bleachers*
*with plastic flowers poking through the holes? Andrew made a*
*face and quickly sprinkled Love Bureau powder over the entire*
*sorry sight. Voilà! A silvery spider web fabric disguised the ugly*
*rows of bleachers, and for added inspiration, Andrew converted*
*the plastic flowers into real ones, long-stemmed red roses that*
*would stay fresh and fragrant the entire evening.*

*Andrew heard voices by the door. Any moment now Delaney*
*would step inside to view the gym. It had to be perfect for her. It*
*had to glow and sparkle with romantic expectation and promise.*
*A night to remember at the Valentine Ball. A few more touches*
*here and there—converting the clunky papier-mâché pillars on*
*loan from the drama department into elegant marble, transform-*
*ing the grade-school hearts and doilies pinned to the wall into*
*frothy concoctions of pearls and lace—and Andrew was satisfied.*
*He made one last sweep around the room, adjusting the lighting*
*. . .*

. . . just as Mitch and Pammi stepped inside the door,
Delaney and the rest of her friends right on their heels.

"Now don't expect too much," Delaney was saying, but
trailed off as she caught sight of the gym. Along with the
others, she stood absolutely still, staring unbelievably at
the vision that sparkled before them.

"Oh, my word," Delaney whispered. Beside her, Mitch
groped for Courtenay's hand.

It was something out of a dream, or a fairy tale. The
ordinarily drab gym glistened like an old-fashioned
Christmas tree, resplendent with tiny gold lights strung
magically from the velvet night sky of the high ceiling.
Iridescent, gossamer-sheer netting hung from the corners

and delicately covered the bleacher section. Little tables set up around the dance floor were haloed by candlelight, perfect for romantically inclined couples who wanted to sit out a dance and perhaps steal a kiss.

Courtenay sighed, breaking the silence. "You call this nice?" she asked Delaney. "You rate this as pleasant? And I thought I was the negative one!"

Delaney looked at the gym in dazed incomprehension, failing to notice the bumblebee that swung merrily from one of the streamers a few feet from her face. She felt an exhilarating surge of happiness and anticipation. It was going to work. The Valentine Ball had to work, judging from the wondrous atmosphere of the room.

"I can't believe it," she said in a whisper. "But unless it's only a magic spell, I have to. I really have to."

*"Oh, it's a magic spell, all right,"* Valentina *pronounced in cold fury, leaping to her feet in the monitoring room, "and I know who's responsible. That infernal idiot of a moonstruck cupid, Andrew! He knows the rules. He listened to me state 'no magic' on this mission, but he ignored my commands and did exactly as he wished. Well, I won't have it. I tell you, I won't have it."*

*She reached for the automatic spell-destruct button on the console.*

*"Please, Valentina, wait!"* Passionata *lifted beseeching eyes to her superior. "It's not Cupid Delaney's fault that there's been magical interference with Woodside High's dance. Couldn't you give her some time? Give the students time to enjoy the Valentine Ball? It's only good policy for the Love Bureau, really. All that emphasis on moon, June, and feelings of the heart."*

*"That's right,"* Enchantée *chimed in, sensing Valentina's hesitation. "Why, the entire population of the school may very well*

138

*turn out tonight, and who knows how many infatuated converts you'll make after Storm Devrie sings his love song."*

*"If he shows up at all," the goddess growled. But she did not push the destruct button.*

*"Don't you want to see how it all turns out?" Bella Rosa pleaded, her nervous smile wilting under the direct gaze of the goddess. Valentina stared first at the dark-haired Senior Sweetheart member, then at each of the other two in turn.*

*"Well, well, if it isn't Delaney's fairy godmother fan club. Cupid Delaney has failed more missions than any other trainee on record, has stirred up more trouble, created more problems, turned this hallowed institution upside down and inside out with her shenanigans, and still you root for her."*

*The goddess paced furiously, deliberating a minute, then flung herself down before the video screen. "I'll give her until nine-thirty. Two hours. No more, no less. But at the end of those two hours, at nine-thirty precisely, the curtain descends on Cupid Delaney and her foolish friend, Andrew. At that time I'll give her the verdict on her assignment."*

*"But what have you decided?" enquired Enchantée.*

*"You'll just have to wait two hours to find out."*

*Exchanging worried glances, the three Sweetheart members crowded around the video screen . . .*

. . . as Delaney came to her senses, blinked down at her watch.

"I don't know about the rest of you, but I've got a dance to coordinate. And in about thirty minutes, kids should start arriving."

She grinned at her friends, her heart soaring like a helium-filled balloon.

"I can take a hint," Mitch said. "I'll start setting up the equipment. The guys in the group will be here any moment, I promise."

He and Courtenay moved off to the stage while Pammi and Tim began setting up the punch bowl and refreshments. Alvin rounded up the chaperones and volunteers as they arrived, and Helen manned the ticket table. By eight-thirty the gym was crowded, and still more students clustered by the door, waiting to buy tickets. Delaney floated through the evening, supervising activities, unable to keep a grin off her face. The Valentine Ball had really taken off, and her classmates had fallen under the spell of the extraordinary decorations and lighting. Mitch and his band were all set to play, but Delaney advised them to wait until Storm Devrie arrived. In the interim, she had a tape of Storm's album going full blast, priming the kids for the real thing.

"Hey, aren't you ever going to slow down and take a break?" Pammi called out as Delaney cut through the dance floor to check on ticket sales.

"Who has time?" Delaney retorted, glancing around at Pammi and Tim, who were slow dancing and smiling into each other's eyes.

"Make time!" Pammi ordered. "Get Alvin to dance with you."

But Alvin was sitting with Helen at one of the candlelit tables. They had their heads bent together and were laughing and enjoying each other's company. Delaney stared at the cozy scene with a pang in her heart. She had been so busy supervising the Valentine Ball, making sure it was going smoothly, that she hadn't once taken the time to stop and enjoy it. Delaney glanced at Alvin, then quickly around the jammed outskirts of the dance floor. But who would she enjoy it with? This was her last social event at Woodside High, and she was literally on the outside looking in. This wasn't the way she had envisioned her final hours as a teenage girl.

There was a stir at the front door. Claire and her select group of seniors entered the gym as if they were royalty attending a peasant's birthday party. The Spirit Club president stood with hands on hips, surveying the goings-on of the dance with a disdainful expression on her face.

Delaney wanted to avoid the girl, but Claire spotted her and beckoned her over with an imperious crook of the finger.

"I come on wingèd feet, thy majesty," Delaney muttered under her breath, but managed a polite smile upon greeting Claire.

"Looks like a nice evening," Claire observed, glancing around, "but I fail to see your promised entertainment. Or is Storm Devrie hiding out somewhere and I've missed him?"

"He hasn't arrived yet."

"Oh, my." Claire raised an eyebrow. "He isn't here yet. But it's a little after nine. What time *is* your star making an appearance so I can be ready with my autograph book?"

Delaney swallowed. "I don't know."

"She doesn't know." Claire smiled smugly at her friends.

"But soon," Delaney said with more conviction than she felt. "Very soon now."

"Hmm, soon. How conveniently vague. Just don't be too crushed when *soon* turns into *never*. Now, then," Claire turned to the clique of seniors, "what do you say we head over to the country club where a real party's going on? I've seen enough at this dead dance to know it's not going to get any better. Not when the major attraction isn't putting in an appearance."

The others mumbled their assent and began to turn to

the door, when someone standing outside shouted excitedly.

"Whatever is going on?" Claire muttered.

Delaney heard more cries as others dashed outside to see what the ruckus was all about.

"It's Storm!" a girl shrieked, wheeling back inside the gym with a glazed look in her eye. "Storm Devrie's coming!"

"Storm!" The crowded gym reverberated with the sound of his name. Delaney felt a rising excitement within herself as well. Her lips twitched a little as she glanced over at Claire, who looked decidedly put out. She beckoned to her friends.

"Well, I'm not staying, that's for sure. We'll have a much better time at Daddy's club. With better entertainment, too. Come on."

No one followed Claire as she strode to the door. Her group of friends remained in a silent huddle, exchanging guilty but excited looks. Claire wheeled about when she realized the situation. Her followers would rather follow the rock star.

"You can't be serious," she said in a withering voice. "How can you possibly want to give up one of my parties for—"

Her words were swallowed up in a thunderous roar as Storm Devrie pushed past her into the gym, surrounded by his own entourage.

# What an Ending, by Venus!

Storm wore an oversized black jacket, white shirt, string tie, and baggy pants. His normally boyish mane of hair had been slicked back for a sexy, hard rock look. The kids drank in the sight of their idol and went wild, cheering, clapping, and whistling.

Delaney smiled sweetly at Claire. "Excuse me. I must go and welcome Storm. Did you mention something earlier about getting him to sign an autograph book . . . ?"

Claire started to say something, then changed her mind. Wordlessly, she stalked out the door, with one backward glare for her traitorous friends, who were jumping up and down and screaming Storm's name.

"Storm! I'm so glad you made it!" Delaney pushed her way to the star's side and looked at him with shining eyes.

"I told you I'd be here," he said. He gave her a quick hug and kiss on the cheek, and the crowd responded with more cheers and cries. Then he turned to the people who surrounded him. "Hope you don't mind, but I brought along some of my own musicians, my press agent, a photographer, and a bodyguard."

Quick introductions were made, but they barely sank

into Delaney's dazed brain. Then she introduced the supervising teachers and the principal, who pumped Storm's hand so enthusiastically the handsome star winced.

Mindy Cohen, Storm's press agent, approached Delaney. "How would you feel about some pictures being taken? Storm mentioned you had a fan club, the Saturday Night Dream Club. Could we get a shot of the members of your club and Storm?"

Could they? With pleasure, Delaney thought. A giggling Pammi and Courtenay and a shy Helen were herded together, and several pictures were taken with Storm, and the names and particulars of their club written down.

"All right, last shots, the four of you dancing with your dates while Storm sings. Everyone come to the stage."

From exhilaration to indecision and depression. Storm strode to the stage and introduced his musicians to Mitch and the members of his band. It took some time for everyone to get set up and discuss arrangements. While Pammi and Helen went in search of an embarrassed Tim and Alvin, and Mitch stepped down off the platform to join Courtenay, Delaney had a quiet moment in which to think. The happiest, proudest moment of her life was turning into a nightmare. In another few seconds she had to make up her mind about Alvin. It was obvious that he cared about Helen and that Helen cared about him. But was Alvin still technically Delaney's boyfriend? When the music started and Storm sang "Dream Only of Me," who would be dancing to the ballad? Tim and Pammi, Mitch and Courtenay, and Alvin and—? Her mind drew a blank, although her heart told her the answer.

Delaney watched the photographer assemble her friends in front of the stage with Storm in the background

*144*

and then scratch his head in confusion over finding one extra girl.

"Well, now," the photographer said, staring at an embarrassed Helen, a mortified Alvin, and a pink-cheeked Delaney, "help me out here. We want to have you four girls with your dates, but which girl goes with this boy?"

There was a tense silence. Helen shot Alvin a despairing look and tried to slip away, but Delaney stopped her. She led Helen over to Alvin and placed her hand in his. Through the lump in her throat she said, "Isn't it obvious? These two go perfectly."

The photographer looked flustered. "But who's your date?"

"I am," came a quiet voice behind Delaney.

She wheeled around to find the mystery boy looking down at her, his yellow brown eyes smiling, his golden hair almost luminescent under the magical overhead lighting. He wore a white sports jacket and linen slacks and a tie emblazoned with little red hearts, and he was the most handsome male in the entire room.

"Shall we dance?" He held out his hand and, after a slight crackling pause, she took it. A thousand firecrackers exploded. Her heart jumped a foot and lodged flutteringly in the back of her throat. What was happening to her? She had never felt this way in Alvin's presence. What was it about this boy, this total stranger, that had her electrified?

The music started. Storm stepped up to the microphone. Her friends began to dance. Slowly, enveloped in a euphoric haze, Delaney went into the blond boy's arms. They began to move in time to the music. The photographer snapped pictures, but Delaney didn't notice how many he took or when the other couples in the gym joined them on the dance floor.

This is perfect, she thought. Absolutely the most romantic night of my entire life as a mortal being. She peered up into her partner's face and was rewarded by a gentle smile that warmed her heart.

"Are you enjoying this?" he asked in a soft voice.

*Up above in the monitoring room, Valentina rose to her feet.*

*"Don't enjoy it too much, little cupids, because your time is up. You've had your two hours. And now you must pay the price."*

*"Oh, no, Valentina!" Passionata cried. "Don't spoil it now! Delaney's having the time of her life. And so is Andrew."*

*"Look at them, Valentina," Bella Rosa said with a sniffle. "Don't they make the cutest couple?"*

*"Silence!" roared the goddess. She pointed a finger at the screen and murmured the magic words and . . .*

. . . the lights in the gym began flickering crazily. Delaney felt the boy stiffen, heard him cry, "Not yet!" as a mighty wind suddenly slammed through the doors and howled around the circumference of the gym. When the noise and excitement died down, everything and everyone had been frozen as still as the castle in "Sleeping Beauty." Everyone except for a shaken Delaney and a fat bumblebee, who buzzed in an agitated manner.

"What—what's going on?" Delaney cried. Realization hit her just as she heard Valentina's sharp and angry-sounding voice coming from above.

"Your time is up, Cupid Delaney. Your mission is officially over."

Delaney fought back tears. "But it can't be! I have until midnight, don't I? And what did you do to the boy I was dancing with? He was right here a few seconds ago and now he's gone!"

She heard the goddess laugh. "You're mistaken, Dela-

146

ney. Your companion is still very much by your side. You're just not seeing with Love Bureau vision."

"What?" Vainly she searched the immediate area, but bumped into the motionless figures of her friends and classmates. There was no sign of the mystery boy. But she did hear humming coming from somewhere over her head, and the mystery boy always had a habit of humming.

"I don't understand," Delaney cried. "What have you done to him?"

"All this concern for a mortal being, a boy you'll never see again, and yet you don't ask a single question about your mission and your future."

Delaney swallowed. It all came down to that, everything she had worked for for the last two weeks, and yet now she didn't want to learn if she had passed the test and earned her wings. Once she knew that, it would be all over for her as a teenage girl, and she wasn't ready, no! She wasn't ready at all to leave behind Woodside High and her life as a mortal.

"Cupid Delaney," Valentina pronounced in the somber tones of a judge, "there have been problems with your assignment since day one. There has been magical interference, and that alone should disqualify you from this mission."

"Magical interference?" Delaney's jaw dropped. "But—but that's not true! I didn't use any of my Love Bureau powers during these last two weeks."

"Yes, I know you didn't, but the cupid I ordered to oversee your mission did. And that is why I'm in such a quandary over this case."

"A cupid observed me? A cupid followed my every move?" Delaney felt herself growing angry. "How dare

*147*

she interfere with my assignment? How dare she use magic when none was needed?"

"It's not a she," Valentina said. "It's a he. Andrew, time to materialize and face the music."

There was a pause. A bumblebee streaked past Delaney's astonished face, creating a trail of iridescent smoke that temporarily obscured her vision. When the smoke cleared, however, the blond boy stood right next to her, a sheepish grin on his face.

Delaney screamed and jumped a foot.

"Cupid Delaney, meet Cupid Andrew," Valentina said in a dry voice.

"But this can't be!" Delaney sputtered. "He can't be a cupid!"

"It can and he is. But whether he remains an emissary of the Love Bureau is another matter entirely. I really don't know what else I can do except suspend him. And as for you—"

Thunder crashed high overhead, drowning out Valentina's words. A brilliant green flash of lightning crackled across the ceiling of the gym.

"It's the Great Goddess herself," Delaney said in an awestruck whisper.

Andrew groaned. "She's probably going to strip me of my wings personally." He and Delaney exchanged bleak glances.

"I really didn't mean to hurt you or your mission, Cupid Delaney," Andrew said. "I just wanted to help and, well, I ruined everything. I'm sorry."

Without hesitating, Delaney reached over and took Andrew's hand. "We'll just have to face Venus's wrath together."

But the face that peered down at them through a mass of pink clouds was not particularly wrathful or upset. If anything, the perfectly proportioned lips curved upward in a mischievous smile.

"Cupids Delaney and Andrew, greetings." The voice was low-pitched, melodious, the tone welcoming. Andrew and Delaney held their breaths, not daring to hope.

"Before you begin, Your Greatness," Valentina interrupted, "I don't think you quite understand the background history on Cupid Delaney, the trouble and scrapes she's gotten into. I must inform you—"

"Silence." One word, uttered quietly, but with authority. Valentina instantly subsided.

The Great Goddess continued. "I want to institute a new program called the Cupid Consultants, and I think Andrew and Delaney would be just perfect for it. The Cupid Consultants will be half-mortal, half-celestial beings, with the hearts, minds, and bodies of teenagers, but the powers and skills of Love Bureau emissaries. The consultants will travel as needed to troubled schools, to work their magic on romantically deprived or hardened students, just as you two did so remarkably at Woodside High."

Delaney's spirits soared. "You mean Andrew and I would be teenagers . . . forever?"

Venus nodded. She smiled gently at Delaney. "Isn't that your fondest wish?"

Delaney sighed. The Great Goddess had indeed read her heart correctly. That had always been her greatest desire, to remain a mortal, and now to be a cupid, as well . . . That was the perfect solution. A dream come true.

Delaney peeked across at Andrew, praying he'd feel the same way. She had no reason to worry. Andrew was beaming idiotically, practically humming in gleeful spirits.

"So it's settled then?" Venus asked. "You're to be my very first Cupid Consultants?"

Delaney and Andrew nodded, unable to stop grinning at each other. But then Delaney remembered the spell, the motionless classmates who filled up the dance floor and gym. And there was Storm Devrie, frozen at the microphone, mouth open in mid-warble.

Hesitantly, she glanced up. "What will you do about the Valentine Ball?"

Venus laughed, a sound like pealing bells on a frosty morning. "Why, let it proceed, by all means. And you two stay as long as you like and have a wonderfully romantic time."

Andrew squeezed Delaney's fingers. "Oh, we will. We definitely will."

There was another rumble of thunder, a crackle of lightning, and the Great Goddess disappeared—just as the entire gym came to life. Without a pause, without missing a beat, Storm continued to sing "Dream Only of Me."

Andrew smiled down at Delaney, held out his arms. "Care to dance?"

"We have to," Delaney murmured, returning his grin. "They're playing our song."